Claire breathed deep in an attempt to loosen the knots in her belly.

Nicolas appeared to know what he wanted from his life and was going for it. He'd treated her well on Friday night, and made her feel special by being genuine. Not the sort of man who'd take what he wanted and walk away from the consequences. Then there was the kind way Nicolas had treated the kids when he was Santa, suggesting he cared about children and their feelings. Add in his suspicions about the boy she was about to see, and he was winning more points by the day.

He's winning me over too easily.

Something that never happened because she refused to allow it. She was on guard with her feelings all the time. She had to protect herself and Mia. Except Nicolas seemed to be overriding all her barriers in one swoop. How come that didn't send her running from the building? Thinking back to Friday night, a tingle of anticipation repeated itself. Excitement was possible if she opened up a little, relaxed and went with the heated sensations Nicolas caused.

Dear Reader,

When Claire McAlpine meets a man who ticks all her boxes but she can't open her heart, what is she supposed to do? She has a daughter to protect too. Nicolas Read has been hurt once too often to trust any woman and yet the new doctor just won't leave his heart alone.

When Nicolas turns up as Santa for the preschool, he is blown away by one little girl's request. He's even more knocked off his feet by her mother. When it turns out he's giving this stunning woman a ride to his work Christmas party, he's sunk. They spend most of the night together.

Over the weeks leading up to Christmas and then on to New Year, they date and slowly open up to each other. But Claire can't let go of her fears of another relationship going bust, and this time it would be worse. Her daughter's heart is at risk too.

Nicolas wants to trust Claire, wants love forever, with a family as well, but he's afraid of being hurt again.

Can these two make it happen? Is the future they both dream about possible?

Read on and enjoy seeing how they solve their problems and overcome their fears.

Sue Mackay

SINGLE MOM'S NEW YEAR WISH

———

SUE MacKAY

HARLEQUIN
MEDICAL
ROMANCE

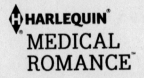

HARLEQUIN®
MEDICAL
ROMANCE™

Recycling programs
for this product may
not exist in your area.

ISBN-13: 978-1-335-73761-8

Single Mom's New Year Wish

Copyright © 2022 by Sue MacKay

Harlequin Enterprises ULC
22 Adelaide St. West, 41st Floor
Toronto, Ontario M5H 4E3, Canada
www.Harlequin.com

Printed in U.S.A.

Sue MacKay lives with her husband in New Zealand's beautiful Marlborough Sounds, with the water on her doorstep and the birds and the trees at her back door. It is the perfect setting to indulge her passions of entertaining friends by cooking them sumptuous meals, drinking fabulous wine, going for hill walks or kayaking around the bay—and, of course, writing stories.

Books by Sue MacKay

Harlequin Medical Romance

Queenstown Search & Rescue

Captivated by Her Runaway Doc
A Single Dad to Rescue Her
From Best Friend to I Do?

Reclaiming Her Army Doc Husband
The Nurse's Secret
The GP's Secret Baby Wish
Their Second Chance in ER
Fling with Her Long-Lost Surgeon
Stranded with the Paramedic

Visit the Author Profile page
at Harlequin.com for more titles.

This is for my girl. Love you.

**Praise for
Sue MacKay**

"Overall, Ms. Mackay has delivered a really good
read in this book where the chemistry between this
couple was strong; the romance was delightful and
had me loving how these two come together...."
—*Harlequin Junkie* on
The Italian Surgeon's Secret Baby

PROLOGUE

SANTA SMILED AT the boy climbing onto his knee. 'Hello, young man. What's your name?'

'Jarrod, and I want a bike for Christmas. It's got to have lights and a bell and bags for carrying my stuff.'

Nicolas Reid stifled a groan. Another kid with high expectations of Father Christmas. It was normal, but wasn't there any kid out there who wanted a toy train or a doll that didn't come with every bell and whistle that had been invented? If he had children he'd want them to be happy, but not expecting to be given anything and everything they asked for. He'd be a bit of a softie, but they wouldn't win every demand they made. Surveying the room, chock-full of excited children, longing flared. A family of his own. Wouldn't that be the best Christmas present he could have? Wasn't happening.

'Santa?'

'What colour bike would you like, Jarrod?' Why had he let Evelyn, his best mate's wife, talk him into getting decked out in stinking-hot clothes in summer—not even thinking about the fake beard making his chin itch—to sit here being tripped over, elbowed, and hearing 'I want, I want' a gazillion times?

'Black's a cool colour.'

'You reckon?'

The kid looked at him and grinned. 'Yep. Can I have a black helmet to match?'

'I'll put it on the list, but I can't promise you'll get what you've asked for. I haven't got lots of bikes in my shed.'

The boy leaned closer and said quietly, 'Mum can hear me telling you what I want and she'll get it.'

Cheeky little blighter. Nicolas found himself smiling at a memory of saying much the same thing to Santa when he was little. He glanced across at the man and woman standing to the side of the plastic fence surrounding Santa's seat. They were smiling and taking photos of their son sitting on the decorated stool beside him, no doubt to be framed and put on the wall. 'Okay, Jarrod, time to give someone else a turn. Merry Christmas and ho-ho-ho. Here's a candy stick.'

'Merry Christmas, Santa.' The boy slid off

the stool and ran across to his parents. 'Santa's cool.'

Nicolas looked to the line of youngsters waiting their turn to tell him what they expected to find at the end of the bed on the twenty-fifth. These little guys were having the time of their life at the preschool Christmas party and talking to Santa was the highlight of their day, while all he could think was how many more kids were in the line. Was he jaded, or what? What about getting over his distrust of women brought on by his ex, and find someone to settle down and have a family with? He'd love a brood of his own kids. Unfortunately he'd learned it was safer going with a light and fun lifestyle. No power punches to the heart.

'Hello, Santa.' A shy voice brought him back to what was important today—making the little kids happy.

'Hello, young lady. Do you want to talk to me from there or are you going to climb up on the stool beside me?' Not every child was keen to do that, and he respected their choices.

'Can I sit on the stool?' the cute little girl dressed all in pink asked.

'Of course you can. Use those steps to get up. What's your name?' Nicolas asked as she shuffled onto the narrow seat.

'I'm Mia.'

'Mia, what would you like for Christmas?'

She looked beyond the fence, and Nicolas's gaze tracked in the same direction to land on a brunette beauty watching the child, presumably her daughter, her face full of love. Love that struck him hard. It was beautiful, uncomplicated, with no expectations whatsoever. What was it like to be on the receiving end of that? Did she have any to spare? To have a woman look at *him* with all that love would set him up for life, add to his motivation to be the best he could, to share himself. The look in that woman's eyes for this little tot was so special, so deep, it stole his breath away, and made him hungry for love in a way he hadn't known since his failed marriage.

Then Mia leaned close and said, 'I want a cuddle from my daddy.'

Nicolas blinked. Pain knifed his heart. This girl wanted a hug from her father. Not a shiny new bike or a fancy doll's house, but a hug from the most important man in her life. Every child unreservedly deserved to be loved by their parents. The one thing he suspected she was not going to get any day of the week, let alone Christmas Day. He should've been careful of what he'd wished for only seconds ago. His arm inadvertently pressed into Mia's. It wasn't a present he could pretend to consider delivering. What the hell did he tell her? Again he glanced at the mother. Shock had widened her eyes. She was obviously used to hearing her daughter's quiet voice in noisy places. She looked at him, gave a desperate shake of her head. Which didn't help his predicament. The one thing he wasn't going to do was promise to deliver a hug from a father who obviously wasn't in the picture. But he didn't know how to answer the child without adding to her pain.

'Santa?' Mia was staring at him with big brown eyes, hope dying right before him. 'Can't you get me what I want?'

His heart squeezed tight. Of all the requests he'd had in the last thirty minutes, this was the one he really wanted to make happen, and the one he couldn't deliver a promise on. 'Let me see what can be done, Mia. It's not an easy present to find.' He mightn't know how, but hell, he wanted to make her smile with happiness.

'Mia, tell Santa about the doll's kitchen you want.' The mother now stood a metre away, her gaze fixed on her daughter, worry staining that love.

The little girl exhaled a slow sigh, making him want to hug her to remove the sadness.

'A doll's kitchen, eh?' Nicolas said, relieved

to have a prompt. 'Are you going to cook for your dolls?'

'Don't be silly, Santa.' She gave him a little smile, while the sadness still lingered in her eyes. 'It's a pretend kitchen so I will pretend to make breakfast for my favourite dolls. There will be pots and plates and spoons too.' She was off and running, excitement beginning to light up her eyes. 'I can't wait.'

'Have you got a favourite colour?'

Mia tapped her chin with one finger. 'I think pink.'

Nicolas glanced over to the mother. The love in her expression as she watched her daughter made his heart pound with a mix of envy and sadness. This woman adored her girl. His parents used to look at him like that when he was a child, but it had faded some as he grew up and didn't follow their dreams for him. They didn't stop loving him, just not as openly, and never as freely as they used to. 'So a kitchen?' he said loudly to get confirmation in case he'd read the situation all wrong and the mother had only been trying to divert Mia from wanting her father.

The woman nodded once, firmly. Her dark brown curls were cut in a bob that finished below her ears, where a set of opal earrings swayed against her cheeks when her head moved. Captivating.

'Santa's going to get your present arranged for Christmas.' Fingers crossed her mother managed to get one at this time of year. The shops were crazy busy already. He didn't want to end this but there was a line of impatient kids waiting and he had no reason to continue talking to a little girl who wanted her father's love, and whose mother had him wanting to know more about *her*. 'Here's a candy stick. Merry Christmas, ho-ho-ho.'

'Thank you, Santa. Please put the kitchen at the end of my bed.' The child slid off the stool and ran to her mother.

Nicolas watched Mia wrap her arms around her mother's legs and gaze up at her. 'I'm getting a kitchen for my dolls, Mummy. Santa said so.'

'Did he? That's awesome.' The woman glanced over at him, her love for her daughter back in place. 'Thank you,' she mouthed.

'No problem.' He looked away. Falling deeper into the gaze that was meant for her girl, not him, would be pointless. He wasn't in the market for a relationship, even if it turned out to be the best thing to happen in a while. His ex had taught him never to give his heart away again, unless he was prepared to risk having it thrown back in his face.

Nicolas beckoned the next child forward, hoping there weren't any more shocks in store. Being a parent must be a lot of hard work, with emotions obviously all over the place at times, but Mia's mother seemed to have her daughter's request under control. Where was the father? Why wasn't he around to hand out hugs? Nicolas disliked the man already. Being there for *his* child would be a priority for him. Always. No matter what else was going on in his life. Unless the man wasn't alive. Could be the reason behind the child's sadness. If only he had a magic wand to make that emotion disappear for ever and replace it with happiness. Likewise for the mother. Her shock had affected him to the point he was thinking about her and his past all at once.

Having children had been on his radar when he was married but his wife was on another page without saying so. They'd been trying for Valerie to get pregnant for months with no luck. He'd suggested they start down the path of fertility tests. That was when Valerie told him she'd been offered a job in another city, and she was taking it. It had been a shock, but he'd listened to her enthusiasm and figured he could forget what she'd done. Her career in interior design was just starting out but already she'd been doing well. They were married. That meant supporting each other, so when he said he'd start looking for work in the same city she was heading to, Valerie shocked him further. She told him she'd begun an affair with a guy working at the company she was going to and she didn't want Nicolas in her life any more. The other man was her new love. That was when he'd also learned she hadn't stopped taking the pill, had only said so to stop him talking about them trying for a family. So much for believing in love and being on side with his wife. Turned out he'd had no idea who this woman really was. He'd trusted her too easily.

'Hello, Santa. Can I have a trampoline?' A young boy stared up at him with wide eyes and a small smile.

Nicolas did the quick glance-at-the-parents thing, and received a sharp head-shake from Dad. 'Come up here and tell me your name first, eh?'

'Can I stay down here?'

'Sure you can.'

The kid relaxed a little. 'I'm Archie. I don't really want a trampoline. I want one of those building sets to make a jet plane.'

'A big plane that swoops down?'

'That's it.'

Nicolas saw head-nodding going on from the parents, and got on with the job of making this boy happy. How many more were there? He could do with a coffee and chilling out with some of the parents he knew from working at the same medical centre. Hopefully that would push away the vision of Mia's mother's face. Lovely when she wasn't looking stunned. Somehow he doubted that image would disappear any time soon. It was so real he had a desire to help her. It was as though there was a connection with her, which was blatantly untrue. Did she feel she'd failed her daughter in some way? He must've failed Valerie somehow if she had to go searching for love elsewhere.

Where was Mia's mother now? A quick survey of the room showed her talking to Joachim, the GP who'd started in the Urgent Care medical centre a fortnight before Nicolas had taken a month's leave to work on his vineyard. Was she a doctor too? Or a nurse? Where did she work? Most of the parents of the children attending this preschool worked at the hospital in one capacity or another. She might be a lab tech or a secretary.

She was laughing at something Joachim said, her eyes wide, and he felt a pang of longing. Which was so unlike him, his brain had to be fried under the hot hat and beard.

'Hello, Santa. What are *you* getting for Christmas?' A lad dressed in an elf's costume stood in front of him, hands on hips with a wide grin from ear to ear.

Nicolas grinned back. It was fun with these kids. Mostly. 'A late morning sleep-in while you're opening your presents.'

CHAPTER ONE

As she drove towards their new accommodation, Claire McAlpine bit down hard on the end of her finger. The tears that had threatened on hearing Mia say to Santa, 'I want a cuddle from my daddy,' were finally leaking down her cheeks. There was no holding onto them any longer now she was alone.

Mia was with Claire's colleague, Joachim and his wife, whose daughter she loved playing with. Far easier to go through the checklist of furniture with the house movers without a little voice interrupting every five minutes. Also a chance for Mia to make another friend. Something she was pretty darned good at, Claire admitted. Didn't get that from her mother. Definitely a paternal characteristic.

I want a cuddle from my daddy. Those words had resonated in her head again and again during the rest of the drawn-out time spent at the children's party. After seeing the shock in Santa's eyes when Mia spoke to him, she'd avoided him once he'd stepped away from his chair, and hadn't relaxed until he'd walked out of the building not long afterwards. For a while she'd worried he'd come back as a normal guy to talk to some of the parents he might know, but as far as she knew he hadn't. He might've confronted her about Mia's request, or tried to be too friendly and kind, which would've made her edgy. It was a private matter. She didn't hide the fact she was single, but it was nobody's business that Mia's father was no-where to be seen. She knew how bewildering and awful it was to grow up without a father, and had never wanted the same for her child. Hearing Mia ask for her daddy's hug had been a punch in the gut.

It was the first time she'd openly said such a thing, and then to a complete stranger. Santa, Claire reminded herself. Santa was the magical man who could bring all sorts of wishes to fruition in a child's mind. His reaction struck her as touching. He'd been stunned but he hadn't passed that onto Mia, instead he'd glanced her way and immediately understood Mia needed diverting. The empathy that had passed from him to her and her girl said a lot about the man behind the fake beard.

'Why haven't I got a daddy like other girls?'

Mia sometimes asked, but never before with such longing. So far she'd managed to divert Mia, saying she didn't know where her dad had gone—which was true—but that she was loved so much she was safe. She couldn't bring herself to tell her girl that the man she'd accidentally fallen pregnant with had wanted nothing to do with his child. Not a thing. He hadn't wanted to know when she was due, or her sex, what her name might be, certainly not her whereabouts once born. Nothing. Today hurt because she'd tried so hard to convince Hank to at least let her send him updates of their child's progress once it was born. His blunt 'No' had said it all.

While pregnant she'd wondered if she was selfish bringing a child into the world with little chance of knowing her father. The sense of loss caused by her own father not being there to watch her ride a bike for the first time, take her to school the day she turned five, to stand and clap when she received her doctor's degree never left her, so how could she put that onto her child? But because of her upbringing she knew she'd be twice the parent her mother had been in her father's absence. Her mother was distant towards her as though afraid of losing her too.

For Mia not to know her father, to never

have met him and not likely ever to, was beyond cruel. As harsh as Claire's father walking out on *her*. Hank had knocked the ground out from under her when he'd held up his hands in a stop sign way when she'd told him she was pregnant, and said, 'Whoa, stop there. I want nothing to do with this. We had a fling, nothing more. Any consequences are yours to deal with. Get an abortion, keep it, whatever. Your choice.'

He'd turned around and walked away, covering his ears with his hands as she'd begged him to stay in touch for his child's sake, not hers. Apparently he'd left Dunedin that same day. She hadn't loved him, or wanted anything from him other than to love their child. She'd known she would keep it, raise and love him or her to bits. She tried to believe she didn't care if *she* never saw Hank again, but the fling had gone on long enough for her to feel safe with him. Something she hadn't felt since the breakup of her long-term relationship with a doctor while she was training. Anthony's dismissal of her had made her feel more unloved than ever, something Hank had added to.

Mia deserved better. Especially unconditional love from the man who'd given her his genes. Hank's words had never left her, though more often than not they were filed away somewhere in the recesses of her mind under the label *Bastard*. On the other hand, Mia had been the surprise of her life, and so worth all the sleepless nights and long days. She loved her daughter to the end of earth and back. She'd do anything for her, including never get so close to a man that Mia became vulnerable. Or her. At the same time, she did have a deep hankering for a loving partner and maybe have another baby. When Mia was a lot older, and *she* was ready to trust again.

If she learned to trust a man not to walk away, breaking her heart, and Mia's, as he went, she might eventually take a chance and cope with whatever came her way without looking over her shoulder for trouble. With her track record it seemed unlikely. Men preferred to walk out of her life.

She had tried to find Hank. Seemed he'd disappeared off the face of said earth. All she knew was he'd come from Britain to New Zealand via any number of countries about six months before she'd met him, and that he was an outdoors man who loved nothing more than mountain-climbing and skiing. He'd explained once, briefly, that he followed his dreams all over the world, never stopping long anywhere, and she'd been enthralled by his sense of adventure. Money hadn't appeared to be a problem, but then they hadn't got into any discussions about anything that didn't involve eating, drinking and sex. Yet the fling had gone on longer than usual for her and she had begun to wonder if he was thinking of settling down.

Once her pregnancy was confirmed Claire had continued working all hours, cramming for exams. She'd become a mother twenty-four hours after she'd finished her final paper. Mia was the best reward imaginable, even better than her qualification. Something she'd never have believed until then. Being a doctor had always been important, so much so that she'd focused on getting through high school with more than high enough grades to get into the pre-med school year at university. Yet one tiny pink, wrinkled little girl had changed everything. For the better. She had someone to love and who loved her back unconditionally. She did not want her child knowing coldness from a father who didn't love her. She knew what that was like all too well. Her father had left when she was four, never to be heard from again. Still she'd tried to track down Hank because his daughter deserved to know him.

Turning onto a side road running between vineyards, she glanced in both directions at the spectacular sight that still amazed her. This was a wonderful district to have come to. They were going to love their new home. Fingers crossed. A small, modern two-bedroom unit she'd signed up to rent, sight unseen, three weeks ago was on the outskirts of Blenheim, close to the hospital. They'd been staying in a motel until the previous tenants moved out.

Excitement stirred in her. Her mother's decision to move to Perth, Australia to live with, and care for, her sister who had cancer, had freed Claire to make a fresh start away from memories of a lonely life growing up with her mother's bitterness and her own pain over her father leaving thirty years ago. Hard to imagine her mother wanting to be with Auntie Jocelyn when they'd only corresponded once a year at Christmas and never talked on the phone, but apparently old age had softened the two women into believing they should be together for this difficult time.

A new start in a location she was unfamiliar with excited Claire. A complete change she'd never experienced and was so looking forward to. She'd chosen sunny, warm Blenheim because it was smaller than Dunedin and seemed very friendly to outsiders and, more importantly, the job on offer was ideal.

Further ahead, a police car with lights flashing was parked across the road. Leaning forward, Claire peered ahead. 'What's going on?'

A cop waved her to stop. Beyond her there were two cars concertinaed into each other so hard it looked impossible to tell where one started and the other finished. Next to them a forklift was slewed on its side across the ditch. Winding down her window, she said, 'Hello, Officer. That looks serious. I'm a doctor. I can help if required.'

'Thank goodness. There're three people with major injuries. Both ambulances are on their way, but in the meantime I'm sure your help will be appreciated,' the policewoman said as she lifted her radio from her belt. 'I'll let the others know you're coming.'

Claire was already out of the car and opening the boot to get her medical kit. 'Both ambulances?'

'That's all we have in Blenheim. If we need another it has to come from Picton or Havelock.'

'At least half an hour away?'

'Yes.'

Claire was met with a scene of carnage as she reached the vehicles, and the sound of screams filled her ears. 'I'm a doctor,' she told the policeman approaching her. 'Your colleague said I might be useful.'

The man grimaced. 'Definitely. We've got two teenage boys in a bad way in the blue car.

They're the ones making all the noise. Neither was wearing a seat belt so they were both thrown around the interior of the car and appear to have some serious injuries. In the sedan there's a woman who seems unconscious and losing a lot of blood from a deep gash in her head. I don't know where you start.'

'Usually we check the silent one first, as that's an indicator of severe head injuries. I'll take her while you see what you can do for the boys. Call me if you're stuck. The sooner those ambulances arrive the better,' Claire said as she stepped across to the sedan.

Peering through what had once been the driver's side window, she saw the woman, lying in a contorted position with her head jammed into the steering wheel. A wide gash was apparent on the side of her face and across her scalp. 'Hello? Can you hear me?' Claire asked, while trying to open the door. It didn't move. Impact had squashed this side of the car back into itself. Glancing around, she found it impossible to tell where one car started and the other ended.

Leaving the door, she squeezed her upper body through the gap. 'Hello? Can you hear me?'

Nothing.

Holding the back of her hand under the

woman's nose, then against her open mouth, Claire felt pops of warm air and saw her chest rising and falling unevenly. Thankfully the woman was breathing, if not perfectly. A good start. Placing a finger on the woman's neck, she found an erratic pulse. The woman didn't stir at Claire's touch. A dark contusion on her forehead suggested she'd slammed into the steering wheel and been knocked unconscious. Claire's fingers found soft areas on the skull near a bleeding wound.

The sound of a siren split the air. Claire remained focused on her patient. The other two victims would have more attention in a moment, and this woman was in a serious condition. Her vitals might be passable, but there was no knowing what other injuries she'd sustained that might've affected the heart or lungs or other internal organs. Internal bleeding was a real possibility, but first to slow the bleeding from the head. Reaching into her kit for a wide crepe bandage and padding, Claire blindly found what she wanted while watching the woman. 'Hello? I'm a doctor. You've been in an accident. Can you hear me?' she tried again.

No response.

Claire sighed. She hadn't been expecting any sort of answer, but she could always hope.

'Hi, I'm a nurse. Nicolas. Do you need a hand here?' A male voice from behind caused her to jerk upward and bang her shoulder against the window frame.

'I've got it.' She pulled out and turned to face the man, and felt a tug in her chest. Tall and broad, he was dressed in jeans that accentuated his muscular frame and a dark blue open-necked tee-shirt that matched the colour of his eyes. 'You might be required to help with the other victims.' Something niggled. Did she know this guy from somewhere? Another quick look. No recollection came to mind and she wasn't blind. Those blue, blue eyes sent a shiver down her spine. That was new.

'The paramedics who just arrived are looking at the boys and said to see what you might need.' He was looking at her with surprise. Why? Feeling the same sense of recognition? But she didn't recognise him, just had a vague sense of déjà vu, and didn't have time to think if she'd met him anywhere. 'One of them will talk to you as soon as the second ambulance gets here.'

'Good. This woman requires evacuating from the car urgently.' She wouldn't have to leave her for a moment. 'She's got a major head trauma. The way she's twisted in the seat makes it difficult to check for internal injuries.' She added, 'I'm a doctor, by the way. Claire.'

'So I was told.' He moved next to the mangled car.

Claire returned her focus to her patient, ignoring the new tingling along her spine. Placing her hands carefully on the woman's head to check for injuries, she said, 'Need a neck brace.'

'Here, I grabbed one from the ambulance in case.' He'd stepped closer, bringing an earthy masculine scent with him. An outdoor kind of smell that brought sunshine and fresh air with it. 'Let's get it in place before trying to get the lady out of the car.'

Claire gently moved their patient's head away from the wheel while the man put the brace in place without hesitation. Experienced, she knew. But still, he had a way about him that said confident and competent. As every good nurse was.

Nicolas elbowed glass fragments from the windscreen, careful not to let any drop on their patient, and tried to ignore the beautiful doctor beside him. Claire, the mother of the little girl who'd asked Santa to deliver cuddles. Guess he had his answer as to her career. She had to be new in town or he'd have come across her somewhere in the small, close-knit medical world of Blenheim. There were shadows under those mesmerising eyes. Working long hours? With a child in tow?

Leaning in, he took the woman's shoulders firmly in his hands. 'I've got her if you want to start moving her upper body.'

'Thanks. There's a trauma injury above her temple that needs a pressure bandage.' Obviously she knew her stuff in emergency situations. 'I need to check her over first. There's more blood under her lower body.'

'I'll hold her steady.' He pushed further through the front and between them, without a word, they moved the woman back against the seat.

'Oh, no. Bigger problem.' Her hands were firm while gentle as she felt around the woman's groin. 'Femoral artery's bleeding. There're bandages in that kit.' She nodded to a bag lying on the ground.

'Onto it.' Nicolas grabbed packets of sterile bandages and opened one to pass to the doctor.

Immediately she pressed hard on the wound to stem the bleeding.

'Want me to do that while you continue checking for further injuries?' he asked.

'Yes.' She didn't waste time on talking, just

waited for him to take over with more large swabs.

Reaching in closer, rose scent wafted past his nose as he placed his hand where hers had been. Glancing around, all he saw was a field of grapevines, not a rose in sight, though often bushes were at the end of the rows to alert growers of disease in the vines. Another, deeper, indrawn breath. Roses and the doc. Again that instinctive sense of connection. Something he did not need. She might intrigue him but he wasn't looking for trouble with a woman. Swallowing hard, he pressed even deeper in an attempt to stop the bleeding altogether until the paramedics arrived. 'Her foot's caught between the accelerator and brake pedals,' he noted.

'We can't shift it without help. Any movement will cause more bleeding.' She wriggled her slim frame to get closer to the woman, and glanced at him briefly. 'Her right arm's broken too.' Something resembling surprise flickered across her face before she continued assessing their patient's injuries.

Did she recognise him? When his face had been covered in a fake beard and his red outfit had been at least three sizes too big? He doubted it.

'Hello, there. I'm Jeffrey, advanced paramedic,' came a voice from behind them.

Claire said over her shoulder, 'We need to get this woman out of here to really see what we're dealing with. Nicolas has the bleeding in check but she needs oxygen.' Then she added, 'I tried prying the door open but it didn't budge.'

Right then a fireman turned up, a crowbar in his hand. 'This any help?'

'You're onto it, Mark.' Nicolas nodded at the guy he'd known since he'd started working at the Urgent Care medical centre and had to treat him for a burn.

Jeffery said, 'Right, Mark, get the door open so we can leverage the woman out. Then Doc, can you finish your assessment while I get the oxygen attached and we can start sorting out her problems?'

'Of course. This one is urgent.' The doctor backed out and straightened up, a grim expression on her face.

'I'd like you and Nicolas to work with me here.'

As soon as the door was wrenched open, the doctor pushed in next to the unconscious woman and reached for the jammed feet, removed the shoes without difficulty or more damage. Her movements were efficient and professional as she checked toes and feet, then moved up the ankles. The kind of doctor anyone would want on their side in this situation. 'Both ankles broken,' she called over her shoulder.

'We haven't done the GCS yet,' Nicolas told Jeffrey. The Glasgow Coma Score would give an indication of how serious the patient's brain condition was. It wouldn't be good considering the woman's head had hit the steering wheel. 'I haven't seen any movement or eye recognition. I'm presuming the score will be low.'

'We'll sort it once she's out and on the stretcher. Right.' Jeffrey surveyed the situation. 'Nicolas, can you keep the pressure on that haemorrhage while we shift her?'

'Someone will have to take over once you've got her off the seat.' He would lie across the mangled front of the sedan where it was scrunched into the other car.

'I'll do that,' Claire answered.

Minutes later she was putting her hand over his, taking up the pressure as he quickly slid away from the wound. No further bleeding appeared. Like they'd practised the move often. He scrambled off the car and took his place beside the fireman as they all lifted the woman onto the stretcher.

'Want me back there?' he asked Claire. 'Or shall I do the GCS?'

'You do it and then we'll swap.'

Nicolas began lifting the patient's eyelids. No response. 'Hello. Can you hear me?' Her mouth moved. When he poked her shoulder she winced slightly. 'GCS of six.'

'Worryingly bad,' Claire said, accepting what he said, not coming across as a doctor who liked to be seen to be in charge.

He liked that. It meant she was more about helping a patient than making sure she was seen to be perfect. He'd worked with his share of opinionated medics, though not so much since he'd started at the Urgent Care medical centre, where everyone seemed grounded and keen to get on with doing what they did best, which was always aimed at helping patients.

Again they changed positions without a glitch. In fact, she barely took more than a glance at him. Which irked a little, he admitted with a grin as the paramedic tightly wound a crepe bandage round the injury he was preventing further bleeding from. Patient first, his ego second.

Claire straightened from examining the woman and glanced at the nurse with his stubbled chin. Did he say his name was Nicolas? She wasn't

sure, being more concerned with the woman
needing help. Sudden, unusual longing for excitement she hadn't looked for since Mia was
born filled her. That deep gravelly voice tightened her skin some. Another unusual reaction.
Add in that outdoorsy scent, and he added up
to quite a package. Seemed she was human
after all if she could get wound up around a
good-looking guy. *Except*, she reminded herself, *my New Year plans don't involve getting
too close to a man.*

'What have you found?' he asked.

Who *did* that voice remind her of? Surely
she'd remember someone who sounded so
nerve-tapping? Pushing the errant thoughts
aside, Claire focused on what was important.
'There's an internal rupture near the ribcage.
I suspect the liver. She was probably thrown
sideways before her head hit the steering
wheel.'

'Anything else?' Jeffrey asked.

'Massive bruising on the left outer thigh.
Impact with gear shift?' It wasn't uncommon
in car accidents.

'As soon as we've got everything in place
we're heading for the hospital.'

'That's good.' Claire felt a weight lift from
her shoulders. She was good at helping injured
people in tricky situations. She'd made it her

go-to place, somewhere she could believe in herself and know she was good enough to be a doctor. But in cases like this the best option was always to have the patient taken ASAP to the emergency department with all the high-end equipment in case something suddenly went very wrong. A real possibility with this lady.

As soon as the patient was loaded, she asked the paramedic, 'Do you want me to look at anyone else?'

'The other crew's got the boys covered, but no one's had time to examine the girl who was driving the forklift, more than ask a couple of pertinent questions. She's in shock, but no apparent serious trauma.'

'Onto it.' Then she'd get back to her car and go onto the house and the movers, who'd be wondering where she'd got to by now. Claire took a quick look at Nicolas and felt another tug in her chest. Why? She didn't usually take a second look at any man. But no denying the unfamiliar sensations ramping throughout her body.

He was checking his watch, and winced. 'If I'm not needed I'm heading away. I'm late for an appointment.'

At five o'clock on a Friday afternoon?

Drinks with his mates? A hot date with a beautiful woman?

Claire McAlpine, get a grip. You're behaving like a besotted teenager.

Her shoulders slumped a little. Must be the Marlborough air, warmer and more seductive. Looking across to the girl slumped against the forklift with a policeman talking to her, she said, 'You go. I've got this one.'

'You sure?'

'Yes.' She watched him stride away, those long legs eating up the ground as if he were in a race. Interesting. She hadn't noticed a man quite so blatantly sexy in a long time. Moving here was a much-needed change, would hopefully bring some fun to her life. She hadn't planned on factoring men into her day-to-day activities. A new start with no one to remind her of the past. Eventually she might relax enough to start dating and having a warm, loving relationship that breathed permanency, but she wasn't rushing.

There was plenty to do over the coming weekend. The movers might have unpacked most of her belongings into the unit, but there'd be all the kitchenware, clothes, toys and bathroom bits and pieces for her to put away in cupboards and drawers. Tomorrow night was the Urgent Care medical centre's Christmas barbecue.

Evelyn, another doctor working at the centre she'd started at last month, had insisted she and her husband, Bodie, would pick her up. Her reason being that no one should go to a party alone. It was a nice gesture, though unnecessary. Evelyn was fast becoming a good friend, offering advice and help about Blenheim, where to live and shop, and the best coffee in town, so she'd accepted graciously. All part of settling into her new life.

'Mummy, can I wear my pink dress? I want to look pretty for Michelle.' Mia stood beside Claire, holding her favourite outfit against her chest.

Mia looked pretty in green baggy PJs, but still, Claire got it. Even at four years old her daughter was very feminine—a trait she might've got from her mother, Claire smiled to herself.

'Since it's a special night you can.' Evelyn's daughter was looking after Mia while Claire went to the centre's Christmas function at a winery on the outskirts of Blenheim. Another plus to this area was all the vineyards and their restaurants. Choosing where to move to had been a bit like throwing a dart at the board.

She'd applied for three positions around the country, and accepted the one here because it seemed likely to fit in with being a solo mum, plus interesting and different from positions she'd had before. It had come up just as she'd been about to accept another offer. Apparently the doctor who'd taken the position had had a change of heart and pulled out, leaving the centre with an urgent need to find someone else.

She'd still prefer going alone to the party and be able to leave early, not have to put on her pleased-to-be-with-you face and stay for more hours than she could imagine being fun. Her social life mainly consisted of preschool events, or Mia's friends' birthday parties. For a change, tonight she was going to be an adult, no childish talking allowed. Hopefully she'd be up to speed.

Had she become somewhat withdrawn from reality like her mother had done when her father left? Quite likely. It had been an example of how to move on from a broken relationship. Yet when Anthony left she'd bounced back enough to have a couple of flings, but when Hank did his number on her and their unborn child she'd crawled into a hole and hidden her heart away. Probably way past time to get out there and make more of what was on offer. Being like her mother, crushed for ever by bitterness, looking at the world as though it owed her something, wasn't the sanest option.

'Look at me, Mummy. Aren't I pretty?'

'Yes, darling, you are.' Seeing Mia's happy smile, a thrill touched her. If her daughter was excited to be babysat then she should take something from that, look to enjoying herself, not think about how soon she could return home. She could end up having a fantastic night out, and not want to come home. Sure thing, Claire.

The doorbell blared. Michelle had arrived. 'Hi, Claire. Hey, look at you, Mia. That's a cool dress.'

'Thanks for doing this, Michelle,' Claire managed between her daughter's excited shrieks as she pirouetted for her babysitter.

'No problem.'

Her phone rang. The night had got busy all of a sudden. 'Hi, Evelyn. What's up?'

'Just calling to say we're running late. Bodie's got problems with the irrigation plant.'

'I'll drive and meet you there.'

'No need. I've called Nicolas and told him to pick you up. He's a nurse at the centre, been on leave for a month. He's also a close friend of ours. I'm sure the two of you will get on like a house on fire. He's already left, so should be

on your doorstep any minute. See you soon.'
She was gone.

Nicolas. A nurse. Guess who that was? The
air stuck in her throat. The sexy nurse who'd
set her hormones dancing. Had to be. This turn
of events meant she wasn't slowly moving forward. If she reacted to him as she had yesterday she was racing into a new life.

Her fingers spun the ring on her little finger as she absorbed how her evening had
changed before it had begun. It could still be
a straightforward night out with colleagues, so
she should relax and have fun, but even now
there was a new level of heat under her skin.
Did Nicolas know who she was? Evelyn would
have filled him in enough to know who he was
picking up, but would he have realised they'd
met twice yesterday?

Gorgeous. Claire breathed deep as she looked
at the man she'd opened her front door to.
There was that tugging in her chest again. Definitely gorgeous. Still sexy. 'Hello, Nicolas.'

There was something like an ah-ha moment
in the deep blue eyes fixed on her. 'Hi, Claire.
I figured you might be the doctor at the accident yesterday.'

The strong jawline and soft laughter lines
at the corners of his eyes were as real as her

imagination had teased her with. She refrained from thinking about a body that suggested he worked out a lot. Then it hit her. Those eyes above the white fluffy beard. *I want a cuddle from my daddy.* Her stomach clenched. 'You were Santa.' How could fate do this to her?

'I was, yes.' His smile was soft—and genuine. 'Are you still comfortable coming with me?'

Knock her down. The guy did understanding as well as sexy. She swallowed. Right now she needed the understanding more. 'I'm not denying my surprise. But I did sense something about you at the accident that made me think I might've already met you somewhere. I just never put it all together.' Another breath. They couldn't spend the evening standing on her doorstep chatting about work. 'I'll say goodnight to Mia and grab my bag. Come in.'

Nicolas glanced inside, then back to her. He spoke in a low voice. 'It was a tricky moment but we got through it. Was Mia all right last night?'

'It was as though she'd forgotten all about it. I don't know what to say, except thank you for diverting her onto the doll's kitchen.' *We got through it.* Claire liked him for that, which was odd because anything to do with Mia was hers to deal with. Would he stop at that? Or want to know what brought on her girl's request? In a bid to keep the conversation on the straight and very narrow, she said, 'Mia was happy, talking about Santa's present nonstop.' Hard to believe how quickly she'd moved on. Swallowing a sudden reluctance to share her space even for a few minutes and having Nicolas see Mia again, she said, 'Come in. She's with the babysitter.'

'Michelle.' Nicolas nodded as he followed her inside. 'Evelyn's my closest friend's wife.'

'She's been so helpful and friendly since I arrived here.'

'That's Evelyn. Hello, Michelle. How was your day?'

'Cool, thanks. Did you know I'm working at the chocolate factory over summer?'

'I heard. There wasn't any peanut brittle in my letterbox when I looked earlier.'

'Give me a chance.'

Nicolas's deep laugh turned Claire's stomach to mush. Nothing like a vibrant, deep tone laugh to lift her spirits. Despite who he'd turned out to be, Nicolas seemed to be an okay guy who mightn't torture her with questions about Mia's father. Fingers crossed, in case she was wrong.

'Mia, darling, this is Nicolas. He's giving me a ride to dinner.'

'Hello, Nicolas. You be good to Mummy, all right?'

Again that deep laugh. 'You bet I will. That's a promise.'

More cramps in her stomach.

Then Mia threw her arms around her. 'Goodnight, Mummy. Have a good time.'

So Michelle had won her way into Mia's heart already. There weren't going to be any tears or arguments. A weight lifted as Claire picked up her evening bag. 'Love you, Mia.' She headed for the door, not giving Mia time to change her mind about being happy for her mother to go out.

Nicolas followed, obviously aware of the need to leave quickly. Claire wasn't surprised. Santa had been fast to check with her about Mia's present. The nurse had been on the ball with the woman in that mangled car. What else was he quick on the uptake about?

Hopefully not her sudden awareness of him in a way she hadn't noticed any man in a long while. That could be beyond awkward, make her feel like an idiot. They'd be working together and, going by her previous, one and only, real relationship with a doctor on the same ward she was training in years ago, workplace romances could get messy. Anthony had been quick to move on with a nurse she'd worked alongside, rubbing it in that she wasn't special.

I'm not looking for another relationship, she reminded herself as she walked down the path beside Nicolas. Mia came first. No other man was going to let her down. Once was enough for any child to live with. Nor was *she* prepared to be let down. Lifting her chin, she headed for the large four-wheel drive parked in her drive and pretended Nicolas wasn't at all sexy or interesting. Or knew that her daughter had father issues.

CHAPTER TWO

NICOLAS HAULED IN AIR. He was feeling as if—what? As if the ground had disappeared from under him. This woman, Claire—Mia's mother, the doctor he'd be working with, the woman who'd snuck into his dreams last night—was beautiful. Opening the door to his four-wheel drive for her to get in, he struggled to breathe.

And when he did manage to, the scent of roses drifted past him. He dragged in another lungful. A scent taking him back to his childhood teased his sensory glands. Summer and his mother's garden. Nicolas looked around. No rose garden in sight. Back to Claire. Her perfume had teased him yesterday, and now it brought on nostalgia for a straightforward love and acceptance from those who mattered. A love he hadn't known for so long he'd wondered if it was all in his imagination. Had to be.

After Valerie had packed her bags he'd gone bush for five days, hiking in the ranges, trying to come to terms with what had happened. It wasn't the first time he'd been hurt. Maddy, his first love, had left him for another man who was always hanging around while he was working on the fishing trawlers. Between Valerie and Maddy, he was left thinking he lacked whatever it took to make them happy. By the time he'd returned home from the bush he was determined to remain single and have the occasional fling when he became too lonely. It had worked up until now. Would continue to, despite the wearer of that scent twisting his gut and making him sit up and take notice of everything about her.

He knew little about Claire, apart from what he'd seen at the accident yesterday, and her devotion to Mia. Yet here she was, stirring him in ways he couldn't explain—or understand. What about a fling? Problem with that was when it was over they'd still work together. Plus there was her daughter to think about. After yesterday he knew Mia was vulnerable and he wouldn't hurt her to have some fun of his own.

Naturally he liked women. There was red blood in his veins. Enjoying sex was normal. Getting close to the woman afterwards didn't happen. It took too much trust on his part to get past the wariness about being vulnerable, something he wasn't prepared to put the effort in for. Could be he hadn't met the woman to make him believe it would be worthwhile. Make him believe *he* was worthwhile.

Claire swung a leg up to get in the vehicle. At least she tried, but her skirt was tight—and emphasised the shapely thighs beneath the light fabric. 'Great,' she muttered.

Taking her elbow, Nicolas helped her up. 'Here you go.' He hadn't considered his vehicle would be awkward for a well-dressed lady to get into.

'Thanks. I'm in.' Her polite smile made him feel awkward.

Why was Claire twisting his gut like this? All he was doing was giving her a lift to the restaurant and he couldn't keep his eyes off her. Or his brain quiet. Keep this up and he wouldn't be able to swallow a mouthful of dinner. Closing the door, he walked around the front of his four-wheel drive, trying to ignore the turbulence his date was already causing. A date with a woman who looked like the friendly girl-next-door when she relaxed—something he hadn't seen too often so far.

'You buckled in?' he asked as he settled into his seat. It was the best he could come up with since his mind had gone stupidly blank except for Claire. The moment he'd slid inside his vehicle the rose garden again filled his nostrils, raising hope for what, he wasn't quite sure. More like, he didn't want to admit to what was causing the tightness in his chest. Physically Claire was his type. Average height, curvy in all the right places, and right now a shy smile that tipped him off-balance in an instant. What was behind that smile? Why shy? Not used to dating lately? If not, they were a right crazy pair.

'All ready to go,' Claire answered. Nothing shy about the steadfast look she was giving him, as if to say, *What else would I be?*

'You been to Grapelands Restaurant before?'

Her light laughter swept over him like a warm breeze. 'I've only been in Blenheim a few weeks. I haven't done any getting out and about so far.'

Just like that, she had him in the palm of her slim hand, wanting to touch her, feel her heat against his skin. *Back off, fast. Aim for friendly, not intense.* 'That won't last now you know Evelyn. Before you know it, she'll have you at every dinner party or event going.' As he well knew. Evelyn, his long-time best friend's wife, was determined to see him settled with a woman who'd make him so happy that he could override his hang-ups from the past, mainly his marriage. She and Bodie had never liked Valerie, and he suspected they weren't unhappy to see her go. Though after putting up with him on many evenings when he was tired of his own company, they might've changed their minds about convincing him to move here in the first place.

'How long have you worked at the centre?' she asked, changing the subject.

Where was the relief when he needed it? A neutral subject should be quietening his stimulated senses. Instead his hands were gripping the steering wheel. 'About four years. I was working at a hospital in Nelson before that, then decided I'd like a change. No more night shifts for one. What about you? You're not from around here, are you?' That was why he hadn't seen those toffee-brown eyes that had filled with love, professionalism and that random shyness before.

'Can't say I've ever missed those either,' Claire said. 'Before moving north I worked at a general practice, which suited me well, what with Mia to look after. The position here is similar, though I do like working with families and getting to know them, so I'll probably go back to family practice at some point.'

'They're always crying out for GPs in Blenheim.'

'Much the same throughout the country. I wouldn't mind setting up my own practice.' Claire was twisting a silver ring on her little finger. Round and round.

Nervous of him? That was a new one. Worried she shouldn't have mentioned going out on her own when they worked for the same company? *Relax, Claire.* He wouldn't say a word to anyone.

'You'd be busy before you knew it.'

'That'd be good.' She was still on edge.

Who had given her that ring? Mia's father? It didn't look like a typical wedding band, but what would he know?

'I think everyone who's not working tonight will be at the restaurant. And even those on shift will turn up after the centre closes. Hopefully not long after eight for their sakes.'

'They're a great bunch. I'm enjoying working with everyone.'

'You haven't worked with me yet. Apart from attending yesterday's accident scene. You might change your mind,' he joked, glad to see her ring finally left alone. A quick glance left and his heart sped up. A lovely vision filled his head. A real woman, not a figment of his imagination. Though he was imagining holding that sexy body against him, running his fingers through those soft curls.

'I've been warned you're a handful.' The shy smile touched her full lips.

Sensual lips that tightened his muscles way too easily. Yes, all of them. 'Thanks.' He drove in silence for a few minutes. Finding out more about Claire seemed important, as if this was his chance to tighten that connection he felt with her. 'Where did you move from?'

'Dunedin. I went from high school to university to med school to a GP practice.' She looked out at the passing vineyards. 'And now I'm here.'

Nicolas couldn't decide if she was happy with that or not. 'Seems to me, you might've been in need of a change of scenery.'

'It was way overdue.'

'I'm a bit the other way, having left home in Auckland at seventeen and never returned. I mostly lived in Nelson, where I went fishing, then enrolled for nursing school.' He flicked the indicator. 'Here's the restaurant.' It had appeared far too soon. Sitting in this cocoon with Claire was charging his batteries. Making him feel good in a manly way. Pushing buttons long out of use.

He pulled into the car park and sighed. 'Let's go and have fun.' The short drive had been fun. Now they had to go mix and mingle with people. The bubble had popped.

Claire didn't move. Her breasts rose and fell on a long breath.

'Claire? I won't hog all your time if that's what's bothering you.' He would make sure she had a good time though.

She turned to him, a wry smile replacing the shy one. 'It's not that. I'm out of practice when it comes to socialising.'

She had to be kidding. But Claire did appear reserved when she wasn't sticking up for her daughter, or helping a woman jammed inside a smashed car, so maybe this was daunting. 'You'll be fine. You know almost everyone and, from what I heard from Evelyn, they all like you. I'll give you five minutes and I bet by then you'll be talking and laughing like the best of them.'

If you're not, I'll be right at your side, encouraging you to relax.

'I can't believe I'm nervous. It's silly.' She shoved the door open. 'Thank you for picking me up.'

His mouth dried. She knew how to get to him without trying. Hurrying around to her side, he took her elbow. 'Any time.'

Claire hesitated again, those big eyes burning into him. 'And thank you for how you handled Mia's request to Santa. I imagine it came as a shock.'

Quit the thank yous. He was only being himself, with a load of intrigue now added in the mix. 'No more than what I saw on your face. It's okay. We got past it.' His arms were fighting to stay at his sides and not wrap around Claire to hold her close and relieve her of the despair creeping over her face. 'That kitchen's going to be well received.' Though probably not as well as the cuddle Mia wanted.

Obviously Claire thought the same because she said, 'It's a diversion, not an answer. But again, thanks. You were great. For the record, obviously I'm single, but there's no ex on the horizon being a pest. It's just me and Mia.' Then a slow blush reddened her skin. 'Sorry, way too much info.'

'It's safe with me.' Happiness flooded through Nicolas, which shouldn't be happening when he wasn't looking for anything more than a bit of fun. And standing this close to hot and sexy Claire was ramping up the fun factor. He'd happily spend time with her, if she wanted the same. But he would continue to play the friendly colleague role and forget what was going on under his skin. Laughter reached them from the restaurant garden.

Saved. 'Sounds like the party's started without us.'

'Better than being first to arrive.' Had Claire realised she'd moved closer to him?

'Hey, Nicolas, good to see you.' Joachim walked in behind them. 'You too, Claire. Jess is inside, Claire. She was hoping you'd be coming.'

The elbow in Nicolas's hand relaxed entirely. Would've been more exciting if he'd taken her hand instead. But he wasn't her date. No one was, he reminded himself. And grimaced with frustration.

'This looks good.' Claire looked around the room they'd entered and smiled at a few people.

'Would you like a drink?' he asked her.

She blinked. 'A drink?' Then she turned on one of those blinding smiles he'd seen when she'd said goodnight to Mia. 'Of course. I'm out and don't have to worry about driving Mia home.'

She really was out of practice. 'What shall I get you?'

The smile widened. 'We're at a vineyard. It'd be rude not to sample their wine, wouldn't it? I wonder if they do a Pinot Gris.' Now her smile was cheeky. How many other smiles did she have? It could be fun finding out.

Excuse me? He wasn't here for that. 'I'll go see. Joachim?'

'Mine's on the table. Claire, come and see Jess.'

Nicolas leaned against the bar, waiting for his order and watching Claire as she chattered easily with Jess. Out in the car park she'd been nervous, yet he'd swear she was already completely at ease now. So her social life had been a bit of a drought. When she was beautiful and kind? Had to be a history there to make her that way. Welcome to his world.

'Here you go.' The barman pushed two glasses across the counter.

'Thanks.' Unable to take his eyes off Claire, he sipped his wine slowly, it would have to last the whole evening since he was driving. Something about her kept snagging his attention. Not something. Many things. Her looks stirred him, sure, but she appeared beautiful on the inside too. Genuine, didn't try to be overly confident when she felt awkward. Though yesterday, helping that woman, she'd been nothing but confident. Seemed to be many sides to Claire McAlpine. He'd barely started getting to know her. The fact he wanted to keep going was disturbing, but he wasn't heading for the door. It had started yesterday when Mia requested that hug for Christmas. Claire's shock and pain had reached inside him, tugged at his heartstrings. It had made him sit up straighter, while wondering who she was and what made her tick. Claire McAlpine was lovely with a capital L.

'You going to stand there all night?' Bodie, his closest friend, laughed, also looking over at Claire.

'No, the wine will get warm.' He'd been so engrossed in Claire he hadn't noticed Evelyn had joined her and Jess. 'Thought you were running late due to problems with the irrigation pump.'

'Got it sorted about the time Evelyn rang you.'

Had Evelyn done it on purpose to set him up with Claire? He wouldn't put it past her. 'That's a relief.' This time of the year the vines soaked up water by the litre. Stepping away, he headed over to hand Claire her glass. 'Pinot Gris as ordered. It's very good, by the way.'

He watched her sip it and saw her eyes widen. 'That's exceptional.'

'You like your wines?'

'I do. I sometimes used to go to Otago with friends for a wine-tasting tour. I have a small collection in my cupboard.'

'No fun drinking alone.'

She said, 'You're welcome to come over and try some.'

The surprise he felt was nothing to the shock widening her eyes. 'I might take you up on that,' he said fast, not willing to give her a way out of her sudden invitation. Visiting with her away from work might fix his curiosity and quieten the noise in his head and chest. *Yeah, sure. Got lots of spare time, have you?*

The grapes in his vineyard were on schedule, and he'd got the bird netting in place during his break so the major projects were under control, but there was always plenty to do. Adding in some social visits would stretch the time budget. Time away from either of his occupations, to relax and enjoy another person's company, could be good for him.

Not that he was lonely. He saw Bodie and Evelyn most days, but having that special woman to laugh and talk with, to share the daily gripes and fun with, would be a bonus. But it wasn't happening. After Valerie, he'd steered clear of involvement, but there were the lonely nights and empty future without a special love to cope with. However, he wasn't filling those nights for the sake of it.

Claire was staring at him. 'We were talking about wine.'

'Yes, I'll see that you do, in the next week or

two.' Damn, but she could distract him. There were women he'd had fun and sex with, but none of them had sparked the deep longing and tightening sensation Claire managed without a blink. Frightening. His heart could be broken all over again if he gave into this need clawing throughout him. *So don't.*

She leaned closer, looking amused. 'Are you always this quiet?'

If only it was appropriate to wind his arms around her and hold her close, to breathe in roses, to tuck his chin amongst those soft curls. 'Make the most of it.'

Her eyes sparkled. 'You think?'

His heart clenched, his breath stuck in the back of his throat. This was getting out of hand. 'How's your wine going?'

Her laugh was deep, and sexy. 'I've hardly started.'

On the wine? Or him? He was in deep trouble if she was referring to him. But she wouldn't be. Until now she'd been quiet, almost shy. It couldn't be him bringing her out of her shell. More likely she felt comfortable surrounded by people she knew. 'Then let's get you going.' Blah. That was bland. Like he was tongue-tied.

The woman Claire had been talking with

looked up at him. 'We haven't met, have we? I'm Joachim's wife, Jess.' She put her hand out.

'Hello, Jess. I'm Nicolas, a part-time nurse at the centre.'

'Part-time?' Claire asked. 'The way everyone talks about you, I thought you must be there twenty-four-seven.' She was laughing at him.

He laughed back. 'Sorry, only three days a week.' Often that equated to thirty-six hours. 'The rest of the time I work on my vineyard.'

'You're a wine-grower as well?' Her eyes had widened slightly and were full of intrigue. 'And I just suggested you try some from my cupboard.' She shook her head.

He had her attention and—admit it—he was enjoying it. His smile faded. Was he setting himself up for a fall? The usual restraints on his emotions were slipping sideways, which was unusual in itself. But one look into those beguiling eyes and he carried on. 'When I moved here I was going to buy a house in town but couldn't get away from how much I enjoyed being out on Bodie and Evelyn's property. It was quiet and the open spaces drew me in, so I bought some land next to them that had been on the market for a while.'

'Was it already established in grapes?'

'Not a vine in sight. But Bodie wasn't letting me languish on the land and I was soon planting vines and putting up wires and posts.'

Claire smiled directly at him. 'Doesn't look like you're sorry.'

'No, it was the best thing I could've done. I enjoy working the land, getting my hands dirty and fighting the elements. But I also love nursing, so it's been a compromise. I sell my harvest to Bodie to add to his, which he then turns into great wine. I'm never without a drop, by the way.' Nicolas felt his chest expanding with pride. For a guy who'd spent the first years of his working life avoiding his parents' demands to get serious and study medicine he'd done more than okay in an unexpected enterprise.

Sure, there were times he regretted walking away from school too soon because the pressure to follow his brother as head boy, then as a top medical student and finally as one of the most sought-after plastic surgeons in the country had ground him down. He'd wanted to be himself, achieve *his* dreams, which were similar to his father's, but he'd needed to do it without the added pressure of being as good as his brother. In the end he'd given up and gone in a different direction.

Which had been successful. First he'd spent years on fishing boats out of Nelson, making and banking a small fortune that he'd used to buy his first house and pay for his years studying to become a nurse. The disappointment on his parents' faces on the day he qualified still haunted him. A nurse didn't compare to a surgeon. Even when they'd given up trying to turn him back onto what they believed was the right track and accepted he was following his own ideas, he sensed their disappointment. If only they'd realised he'd have done what they'd wanted if they hadn't spent his whole childhood comparing him to his brother, because it *had* been his dream to be a surgeon. Not in plastic surgery, but general surgery, which still would've made them proud. Now he was okay with his choices, preferred his lifestyle to that of an overworked, harried surgeon.

'Seems you've got the best of both worlds.' Claire appeared to understand what that meant to him. Because she'd dealt with problems taking her own route through life? Raising Mia alone without doubt would've added to the pressures of working as a doctor.

'I have.' There were still a few worlds out there he hoped to conquer. The most important being to have a family with a woman he loved to bits. Who loved him back. Children he'd never compare with one another, nor set his goals for them to make their lives around. Where was Mia's father? If he'd died, wouldn't

Claire have worded it differently when she'd mentioned no man lurking in the background? So there had to be a father somewhere who apparently didn't show his daughter any affection. But how could a man not hug his little girl? He must've got it wrong. That was beyond comprehension.

'Hello, you two. Enjoying yourselves?' Evelyn asked with a mischievous smile on her face. She couldn't be trusted not to interfere if she thought he needed a kick in the pants to make a move, either about his career or his single status.

'We're doing fine, thank you.'

Claire glanced at him with one eyebrow slightly raised, matching the way the corner of her mouth turned upward. 'We are indeed.'

Evelyn was still grinning. 'I thought it wouldn't hurt for you both to meet before you got here and had no time to talk.'

Soft laughter spilled from Claire. 'You were way behind the ball, Evelyn. We'd already met. Twice.'

'Twice? Where? When?'

'For us to know and you to keep wondering.' Claire sipped her wine. 'You should try some of this. It's excellent.'

Nicolas kept his laughter tucked inside, but the look on Evelyn's face was hilarious. Right now she had no idea what was going on, and he wasn't about to let her off the hook. It was fun seeing her confusion. Point to Claire. He could get to like Claire even more.

'I'll get you a Sauvignon Blanc, shall I, Evelyn?'

'I've got that.' Bodie held a glass out to his wife.

Claire was still smiling. 'Mia thinks Michelle's wonderful. She put her favourite dress on for her.'

'There you go. Hope Mia likes chocolate because Michelle took some with her. The staff are given samples every day.'

'Think I'll get a job there,' Nicolas said. 'They make the best chocolate imaginable.'

'I haven't tried it,' Claire told them. 'I've been buying lots of cherries instead. They're my favourite fruit.'

He watched her sip her wine and his stomach lurched. Her lips were full and gave him tingles just imagining them on his skin.

'I'll be back.' He needed to step away, get under control before Claire saw the need in his eyes. He headed outside into the garden, where the chefs had the barbecues cranked up.

'Here, get that into you.' Bodie handed him a replenished glass. 'You look like you've taken a hit.'

'I haven't finished my first drink.' He took the proffered glass anyway. Now he looked desperate, holding two drinks.

'It's iced water, known to fix dry mouths,' Bodie said. 'I checked your grapes today. They're bang on target for harvest.'

Two months away. Bodie was giving him a chance to catch his breath and get back on an even keel. 'I figured they're coming along as they should.' Harvest was a crazy time with little sleep and a lot of work. 'I've already arranged to hire casual labour for the week it'll take to collect the grapes.' It would be up to him to oversee everything, meaning another break from the medical centre, but he had plenty of leave up his sleeve.

'As long as the summer doesn't turn wet, we'll both have bumper crops.'

'Pinot Gris and Chardonnay to fill the cellar.' They always kept some back to enjoy throughout the year. Claire liked Pinot Gris. Something they had in common.

Bodie was sniffing the air like a spaniel. 'Think the steak's almost done.'

'Let's bring the women out to one of those tables under the trees.' It was a beautiful setting and the night was warm.

'I'll claim one,' Bodie agreed with a cheeky look. 'You round up the women.'

Thanks, mate. Could've given me some breathing space.

But Bodie was on the same page as his wife. The two of them couldn't leave him to sort out his single status. They knew how little he was trying to change his lifestyle. They also knew how one day he'd like to fall in love again, and have some kids to raise and cherish. And that he wasn't just taking it slow, but instead was actively protecting his heart. Someone had to, and who better than him?

Draining the glass of water, Nicolas headed inside. 'Claire, Evelyn, want to join us outside? Bodie's nabbed a table. Jess, Joachim, why don't you come out there too?' Claire looked so relaxed with these people he wanted to keep it that way so she didn't wander off to join another group.

She walked beside him as they headed out to the table. 'This is fun, having adult time and not having to worry about Mia.'

'Do you really not get out without her?' It was hard to believe when she was so vibrant at the moment.

'My friends in Dunedin had a daughter the same age and we took turns babysitting for each other. I'd go to book group and a couple of other groups like that.'

He held back saying she should be getting

out with people who knew how to have light-hearted fun. Instead he said, 'You can do the same here.'

'I haven't had time, what with moving into the house, getting to know the job and settling Mia, though, to be fair, she's been cruisy about the move. Not worried about meeting new friends or having a new bedroom.' Claire's smile was all for her daughter. Lucky kid.

What would it take to get her to smile at him like that? He needed to calm down. 'Throw in the fact it's December and most groups close until February and your timing sucks. But there are plenty of other things to do around Marlborough in summer. Boating, fishing, swimming, picnics.'

She was staring at him as if he were crazy. 'Boating? Fishing?'

'You know? Floating on the sea, a line hanging over the side of the boat, a gentle tug on the hook and winding it in like fury to get the blue cod on board for dinner.'

'I've never fished.'

'You like eating fish?'

'That's what fish shops are for.'

'Then you haven't tasted fish so fresh it falls apart while it's cooking.' A plan was forming as he talked, but he kept it to himself. Too early in the evening to be suggesting they spend a day together on the briny. Or anywhere. She mightn't like him enough, might think he was downright uninteresting and start looking around for somewhere else to sit.

'Can't say I have.' This time her smile was teasing. 'But there are a lot of things I haven't tried.'

'If you think you and Mia would like wandering around the vineyard let me know and we can arrange a time to suit. Kent, Evelyn and Bodie's boy, could join us. Has Mia met him?'

'They go to the same preschool and get on well.'

That made things easier. 'I can take Mia for a ride on a tractor, if you think she'd like that.'

'You'd be making a friend for life. Anything with four wheels intrigues her. I believe she wants to learn to drive my car before she's got the hang of her bicycle without trainer wheels.'

Did that friend for life come with her mother? He always knew when he was onto something or someone who intrigued him. He and Bodie had met at a rugby game and become instant friends. They'd never let each other down in a big way since. The day he'd gone to knock on the door of a fishing company at Nelson Port to make enquiries about work on a trawler, he'd known from the moment he'd been taken on board to look around it was the right job for him to get ahead. When he was first introduced to Valerie, his ex-wife, he'd been hesitant at first. She seemed kind and fun, yet there'd been something about her he couldn't put his finger on. Whatever it was, he'd put it down to the insecurities his family handed him and moved on to fall in love with her, only to have it all backfire a few years later. Something to hold onto so he didn't make a mess of his life again.

'I'd better hide my four-wheel bike. Can't have Mia thinking she can ride that yet.' Four-wheel bikes were involved in far too many accidents on farms.

Claire shivered. 'I've seen the stats, and dealt with a couple of farmers who've come a cropper when out in the paddocks on their bikes. It wasn't pretty in either case.'

'They're one of the best inventions for getting around the land, as long as whoever's on board wears a helmet and doesn't try to overdo speed or steepness on an incline. My land's fairly flat, but I'm still cautious. Haven't got the need to break a leg or worse.' At the table, Nicolas pulled out a chair for Claire.

'Can I get you a refill of wine?'

'Please. More of the same. It's so good being

able to relax and not worry about Mia or getting home.'

'Be right back.'

'That's good.' Claire put down her glass and relaxed some more. It was so easy to do around Nicolas. For a moment there she'd wondered if she should get up and go talk to other people instead of hogging Nicolas to herself. But he was easy to be with. If she didn't focus on the tightening of her skin every time his eyes met hers. Or how her toes seemed to be dancing inside her sassy shoes.

The guy was something else. Toned muscles filled his shirt and shaped his trousers. His hands looked strong and gentle, capable of teasing her awake in a blaze of heat. While his face appeared open she'd seen his muted concern for that woman in the accident yesterday. As for his lips—they could turn her into a blithering idiot with one touch. It wasn't as though she hadn't dated a good-looking man ever before, but it was rare for her to get so wound up so fast. Nicolas was sexy beyond her experience. *We're not on a date.* Shame about that. She might've let her hair down if they were. A short fling wouldn't hurt. And was long overdue.

Another sideways look and her heart hammered. The moment she'd opened her door to Nicolas she'd felt a connection. The cause was probably the Santa incident and working together at the accident scene. She was certainly more aware of him than usual with men she didn't know.

Nicolas leaned closer. 'Word of warning. Now you're friends with Evelyn be prepared to get elbowed in a multitude of situations.'

Claire laughed. 'Think I worked that out already.' Plus he'd already hinted at it. Then that manly scent reached her and she sat back, holding her breath. It was too good. Heated her in places she didn't need right now.

Nicolas was watching her as though reading her mind. He'd better not be. She'd curl up in a ball of embarrassment. Then what he'd said about Evelyn hit home. 'Asking you to pick me up tonight doesn't come into that category—' his eyes widened '—does it?'

Surprise flicked across his face, before he shrugged. 'Honestly, until you said that I didn't think so, but now? Who knows?'

'Great.' Just what she didn't need, someone trying to set her up with a guy. While she'd moved here to break out of the dreary life she had in Dunedin, and to hopefully find happiness with someone eventually, she was not ready. Certainly had no intention of rushing into a relationship until she knew how life here was going to be.

Nicolas was still watching her closely, as though he wanted to find out more about her.

Again she hoped his mindreading skills were poor. Time to put some space between them and let the heat that look instigated cool off. She picked up her glass in preparation to head over to talk to someone else.

Nicolas reached over with his to tap the glass she held. 'Here's to a fun night.'

The air puffed out of her lungs. She didn't really want to go be with another group, with anyone else. She liked sitting here with Nicolas. She was liking him more with each passing minute. Whatever that might mean. A few hours chatting and enjoying dinner. Or more. Taking Mia out to his property as he'd suggested, or a short fling. With all the heat cruising throughout her body, anything could happen. One thing—*no hurting each other, please.* She couldn't take another broken heart.

'Come on, you two. They've put the steaks on the service table,' Bodie called.

Nicolas blinked as though he'd forgotten where they were. 'Coming.' He stood up and made to pull her chair out when she rose. 'Ready for dinner?'

'Absolutely.' The urge to slip her hand in his

as they crossed to the tables laden with salads, fish and vegetable dishes was so strong she had to clench her fingers into a ball. When had she ever done that? She couldn't remember. Had to be eons ago. Reaching out to Nicolas was wrong. The man had given her a ride, not invited her on a hot date. All very well to be excited being with him, and thinking about things she hadn't in a long time, but she needed to know more about him if she was following that path. Truthfully, she wasn't. She didn't want to be let down again. Two men had done that already. They were the reason she was OTT hesitant about getting into a relationship. Too easy to give her heart away, a damned sight harder to put it back together. Anyway, she had to be super-careful for Mia's sake. No man she brought into their lives was going to hurt her girl.

When she was training to become a doctor she'd met Anthony, another trainee, and they'd soon got together as a couple. He'd been kind and generous to a fault, and she'd loved him for it. Then one day when they'd been together almost three years, he'd said he didn't love her enough to spend the rest of their lives together. She'd been devastated, and from then on more afraid than ever to let any man too close. But behind that fear lay a longing to fall in love with a wonderful man and have children. She still wanted those things, but not at the cost of her daughter's trust and love, let alone hers.

Nicolas handed her a plate. 'Here you are. There's an amazing array of food to choose from.'

'My stomach's rumbling already.'

He leaned closer. 'I can't hear it.'

A whiff of his scent teased her again. Nothing like a good male smell to set her hormones dancing. *Down girl.*

'Be glad you can't.'

'What are you going to have?'

'A bit of everything?' She grinned.

Doing a lot of smiling, Claire.

Why not? Nicolas made her happy and brought on the smiles. There was nothing much she could do to stop them. 'I'll start with the steak.'

'Nothing like a good steak cooked to perfection and these certainly look like they are.' Nicolas handed her the servers. 'Here you go.'

The food was excellent, the company even better. Claire sighed happily as they left the restaurant after ten. She couldn't remember the last time she'd enjoyed herself so much. The crowd had thinned out and when Evelyn and Bodie said they were heading home Claire decided it was time for her too. Much as she was enjoying herself—and Nicolas—she was tired. Or was that an excuse to cut the night short before she had to make any serious decisions about where she went from here? Did she invite him in for coffee? A kiss? It wasn't a date, but that wouldn't matter if they wanted to get intense.

Intense. She couldn't risk it. Too much to lose. Her heart sank when it should be standing strong. His easy nature and caring way attracted her, but didn't explain the heat in her veins, nor the tightness in her legs. That was down to sex, nothing else. Even that wasn't happening. Not tonight anyway. And Nicolas mightn't be interested anyway. Though he had spent most of the evening with her, but hadn't cramped her style—not that she had a lot of that. She smiled to herself. She was so out of practice socialising it wasn't even funny any more.

'Did you enjoy yourself?' Nicolas asked as they drove away from the restaurant.

'I did. I feel as though I belong even more now. Being social with colleagues makes the day-to-day grind easier somehow.' Everyone had made her welcome and treated her as though she'd always worked with them. This move was turning out to be better with each passing week. Glancing sideways to the man she'd spent most of the evening with, she shook herself mentally. He was so different to Anthony with his openness and not trying to win her over with platitudes. Hard to imagine him denying her pregnancy either. That excited her. *Careful.* She was reading too much into his straightforward ways. One dinner together— amidst a crowd—didn't make a future. But it had started her dreaming of possibilities.

Put the lid back on the box, Claire. You're not ready for a full-on relationship. You've only just begun this new adventure in Blenheim. Tread softly and slowly or you're going to get hurt.

'I've never thought of it like that, but it makes sense,' said Nicolas.

'You can tell I've hardly changed jobs any more than I've moved towns,' she said with a tight laugh.

'You're glad you've made the move?'

'So far it's one of the best things I've done in a long time. Mia's happy too. Not that she wasn't before, but I did worry she'd find it hard making new friends, but I should've known better.' Her girl was a little toughie, most of the time. Didn't do so well whenever she hurt herself physically. Then she needed hugs and kisses to stop the tears. Nothing wrong in that. Claire loved handing them out any time, not only when they were needed. Only to her daughter, that was.

Men usually let her down. If she was even thinking there might be more to come with Nicolas she had to take it ultra-slowly. Not only for her own safety when it came to her heart, but Mia as well. More so Mia. Her girl longed for a father to love her, cuddle her. She understood how hard it was not to have that, so the absolute last thing she would do was let a man into their lives who wasn't going to stay—for ever. So no hugs or kisses going on tonight. They would've been exciting though.

CHAPTER THREE

NICOLAS'S HEART WAS pounding as he drove away from Claire's after seeing her to the front door. What a roller coaster of a night. They'd got along ridiculously well, while all the time alarm bells had been ringing. Claire was wonderful. He wasn't ready to get close. Claire was wary. He was enthralled. Not to mention cautious.

If only they were in the sack right this minute, making out like he'd been denying he wanted from the moment she'd opened her door to him. When was the last time he'd been so intrigued, felt so much fizzing in his blood? There'd been a connection. He was certain of it. His more wary side was relieved Claire had firmly stepped away from him at the door with a quiet smile. He wanted to leap into whatever was brewing between them. He wanted to head out of town and not stop until the sun came up, bringing some clarity with it.

Guess if Claire was at all interested in some fun then she was being careful. Knowing nothing about her past, he had to accept her move. Even if there was nothing to make her wary of getting close, he understood she mightn't be feeling it for him. Some of her glances his way had suggested otherwise—eyes flashing brief glimpses of hope and longing. If he knew nothing else, he knew she wasn't about to rush blindly into a relationship that could backfire and hurt her and Mia badly. He felt she was worth waiting for. If he was ready to go further—and really there was nothing to say he was—he had to be patient and careful. Even if only for a brief fling.

Could be that he should be grateful to her. Rushing into getting close was not a good idea. He'd taken his time with Valerie and it had still gone belly up. He hadn't been good enough for her. Another man had given her what she wanted apparently, though he'd seemed to disappear from her life shortly after their breakup.

Toot, toot. A car came up behind him as he slowed for his entrance. From the logo on the front he knew it was Bodie and Evelyn. No doubt they'd be laughing their heads off about the fact he was already heading home.

His phone beeped as a message came in.

He braked to a stop and glanced at the screen, then cursed his friend.

Lost your touch, mate????

Evelyn had to be driving since that was Bodie's number. And his wit. He turned up their drive. They owed him a drink for their cheek. He'd walk the couple of hundred metres across the paddock to home afterwards.

'Got a thirst going?' Bodie asked as he clambered out of his state-of-the-art four-wheel drive, a grin on his annoying face.

A larger thirst than a glass of wine would fix, but he'd keep that to himself. 'It's still early. I'm not ready for bed.'

'I bet.' That grin expanded.

Should've driven straight home. Sipping the wine Bodie poured a few minutes later, Nicolas looked around at the family photos on the walls of the lounge, and paused. Evelyn had Michelle ten years before she met Bodie. Her marriage had fallen apart two years earlier and she'd raised her daughter singlehanded until Bodie came along and won her over.

'Do you know how long Claire's been on her own?' he asked Evelyn. He was open to the idea of raising a partner's children, and adding more to the mix. Being a dad was right up there with being happily married. But first he had to find the right woman and, since he hadn't been looking, Claire had blindsided him.

'From the little she's said, I think she was single when she had Mia, and I don't think there's been anyone in her life since then. But you'd have to ask her. It's not for me to gossip.'

'Fair enough. She said very little, but it is early days.'

'So there'll be some days?' Evelyn wasn't teasing. She was watching him closely, as if this was important.

Which it was, if he was to get together with Claire. These two were his closest friends, they knew his past, and how he had to be careful because he didn't think he could face heartbreak again. But others did and were happy. Like Evelyn.

'I hope so.'

If Claire's keen.

She *had* leaned in closer to talk to him a couple of times, cutting others out of their conversation.

They needed to shift the conversation away from Claire. She wasn't here to stick up for herself, or to refute any suggestions they might come up with about who she was. His fault for raising the question.

Evelyn must've had the same thought, because she said, 'You both seemed to get on well, for which I'm glad. So, what's on the work menu for tomorrow? Servicing the harvesters?'

'I've got some spraying to do,' Nicolas answered. Hopefully that would keep him busy all day and his mind off a particularly attractive and alluring woman.

It worked for most of the day, but first he'd had a sleepless night, tossing and turning while his mind kept flipping up images of Claire. Claire smiling. Claire looking shy. Though somehow he suspected it wasn't shyness, more reticence about letting go too much. Then there was the wave of heat she caused in him time and again when he sat near her. Getting down and greasy on the harvesters had been good for him. Checking oil levels, tyre pressures, motor status, had kept Claire at bay. Until he tossed the rags in the bin and headed inside for a well-earned beer and dinner.

Come Monday and work, and Nicolas was keen to pull on his nurse's persona and get to the Urgent Care medical centre. Working in two entirely different jobs gave him a lot of energy and enjoyment. One very physical, and the other more about caring for other people.

'Morning, Nicolas,' Claire called as he stepped into the office, where another doctor and three nurses stood around with mugs of coffee in hand. She looked bright and cheerful, and was smiling widely. Was work her happy place?

'Hello. You had a good weekend?'

'Yes. Finally finished unpacking the last boxes. Took Mia to Pollard Park. Nothing major but all good. What about you?'

If only he could've been a part of her weekend. Though unpacking cartons of her household gear wouldn't have been exciting, the company would've been. Interesting.

Pouring a coffee, he replied, 'Sprayed the vines, mowed between the rows, and had a soak in the hot tub at the end of the day.' With a beer and dreams of a holiday on an island with a sexy lady named Claire. Unbelievable how much of his time she took up just by being in his head. How unusual it was. Scary. As if he'd started on the long, slippery slope to opening up his heart and there was no stopping him. There had to be. He wasn't ready. Might never be.

'That sounds like a lot of work. You're here for a break then.' So she could tease him. Good.

'No break happening,' Tina, the receptionist, chuckled. 'We've already got a queue waiting outside the door.'

'We'd better get started then. I'm triage today.' Nicolas headed to the office to place his coffee on the desk before going to unlock the front doors and start the day rolling. 'Morning, everyone.'

He was greeted with the usual calls of hello and concern.

'Take your turn at Reception. We'll be seeing you in order of priority, so don't feel you have to push ahead of anyone.' It happened all the time, people wanting to get in first. Getting to work on time didn't come before chest pains or suspected fractures. But it was also true that the first patients registered usually were seen immediately as two doctors were waiting to start their day. People with serious injuries or conditions would've gone next door to the hospital emergency department. This centre was for those with less urgent problems or those who didn't have a regular GP to visit.

Back in his office, he hummed to himself as he watched the computer screen and waited for the first patient's name to appear. He'd get that one assessed pronto, then they'd go straight through to Claire or Ryan.

'Thank you again for Friday night,' Claire said from behind him. 'I really enjoyed myself.'

Surprised, he spun around on his office chair. 'So did I. It turned out to be fun.' Standing up, he met her wary gaze full-on. 'I truly enjoyed spending time with you. We should go out together some time.' Sooner rather than later.

She blinked, and her smile returned. 'I'd like that. A lot,' she added in a rush.

'Good. What—?'

'Claire, can you take the first patient?' Ryan appeared in the doorway. 'I've got to go across to ED to sign off some paperwork on a patient I sent them yesterday.'

'No problem.'

Nicolas sat back down and looked at the screen. 'Thirty-one-year-old male, query fractured wrist. You want to take him straight through to your room? I don't need to triage him.'

'Sure.' She came closer and leaned over to read the sparse notes. 'Joey Sanders. Got it.'

Nicolas breathed deep, inhaled roses. The scent was becoming addictive. 'There's the next case coming up.' Go away and take that scent with you. 'Hope Ryan doesn't take too long.'

'Me too.' Finally the roses floated out of the room.

Five minutes and he was already screwed. It was going to be a long day. Shoving off his chair, he headed out to the waiting room. 'Trish White? Come through.'

The thirty-six-year-old hobbled after him and sat on the seat he pointed to.

'I'm Nicolas, the triage nurse. You've hurt your ankle. What happened?'

'I tripped over the cat on the way to the bathroom and went down in a heap on my ankle. I hope I've only sprained it, but it is very painful when I put weight on it.'

'Place your foot on my chair so I can have a look.' Moderate swelling made it difficult to feel anything. 'Did you knock your head or feel faint before you tripped up?'

'No, nothing like that.'

'I'll check your blood pressure in case there's a medical reason for your fall. How did you get here?'

'My neighbour dropped me off at the emergency department on her way to work. I was told to come over here as this isn't considered urgent.' Trish sounded peeved. 'Walking over was painful.'

An orderly should've brought her across in a wheelchair.

'They prefer to keep the department free for serious injuries, and you'd have had to wait longer to be seen there.' BP normal. 'So there's no one with you?'

'No.'

Darn. Always better to have another person to hear what the medical staff had to say. 'Stay here while I get a wheelchair.' Along with a nurse to take her to Ryan's room, since he could hear the other doctor out in the hall. 'Jude, can you grab a wheelchair? I've got a patient for Ryan.'

'Here we go.' Jude rolled a chair in.

Nicolas held the wheelchair while Jude helped Trish stand and swivel around to sit again.

The woman winced. 'It can't be broken if I can limp along on it. I haven't got time for a broken ankle. I'm getting married in two weeks and I don't want to be on crutches for that.'

That explained her agitation. 'Let's not get ahead of things. The doctor will examine your ankle and if he thinks there's a concern he'll send you for an X-ray.'

The next patient was a six-year-old boy with

bruises on his face. 'What have you been up to, young man?'

'I fell off my stool at the table and crashed into my brother's highchair. He laughed. It wasn't funny.'

'Not really.' The bruises were large and red, indicating they were very recent, but Nicolas looked closer and noted patches of green and dark blue around the edges of the new bruises. Older bruises. Something not right here.

'You'll be all right, Noah,' his mother said. 'You shouldn't have been bouncing around on the stool when you were meant to eat your breakfast and get ready for school.'

'But Dad said—'

'Dad said to hurry up or you'd have to walk.' The woman's face was tight, and her mouth grim.

Nicolas asked Noah, 'Did you hurt yourself anywhere else? Your arms or back?'

The boy looked to his mother, then down at the floor. 'No.'

'I'm going to touch your head in places and I want you to tell me if it hurts, okay?'

He nodded, still looking down.

Checking the boy's skull elicited not a sound from him. Nicolas then lifted the boy's tee-shirt and gently felt his ribs and shoulders, down his spine. A couple of old bruises but no pain. So he might be reading more into this than was real. Then a small shudder as Nicolas touched his left side. Something was not right. 'There you go. I want you to sit in the waiting room with your mother for a few minutes. The doctor will come and get you very soon.'

'He's always been accident-prone,' the mother said as she helped Noah off his chair and took him by the shoulder to head out of the room.

Heard that before, Nicolas thought as he went to see if either Claire or Ryan were free to talk to. Claire was at her desk scrolling down the in-patient screen.

'Got a minute?' he asked.

Her head rocked back a bit as he closed the door behind him. 'Have you got a medical problem?'

'Not at all.' Seeing her for medical advice wasn't on. They worked together, and some things were best kept separate. 'I'm concerned about the next patient. Six-year-old Noah has major bruising to his face. There appear to be older bruises beneath today's, and he got uncomfortable talking about them at first, saying he'd fallen off the stool into his brother's highchair. As though he'd been told to shut up about anything else. I could be completely wrong, but my antenna's up and pinging. He flinched when I touched his left side.'

'You're concerned about abuse?'

'See what you think. He tensed up when his mother mentioned Dad.' Nicolas headed for the door. 'I'm probably overreacting, but I've seen this before and would hate to miss the signs. Of course, what happens next if I'm right lands on you, and might add up to zilch if the mother isn't prepared to talk. She appears to be a tough nut to crack, but I've seen them fold before once the questions get too close for comfort.'

'I'm glad you mentioned your concerns. It's hard enough dealing with abuse without having to tread carefully around the parent.' She stood and looked directly at him. For a brief moment he forgot why he was here. 'I'll be on the lookout now.'

It was all he'd asked for. 'Good.' Stepping out of the room, he went back to his room and looked up the next patient.

'Nicolas,' Claire called.

He turned.

'I'd like you to join me with Noah and his mother. They've already spent time with you so we'll do a thorough exam together.' Her shoulder lifted subtly. 'A second opinion is always important in these cases.'

'I'll bring him in now.' His feet were all but dancing as he headed to the waiting room. They were on the same page. Great.

Claire breathed deep in an attempt to loosen the knots in her belly. Nicolas hadn't turned into a frog over the weekend. He was still good-looking in that outdoorsy way, his skin no doubt tanned from working in his vineyard, his stride firm and confident and his head held high. Her kind of man—if she had a type. So far she hadn't done well in that area.

Nicolas appeared to know what he wanted from his life and was going for it. He'd treated her well on Friday night, and made her feel special by being genuine. Not the sort of man who'd take what he wanted and walk away from the consequences. Then there was the kind way he'd treated the kids when he was Santa, suggesting he cared about children and their feelings. Add in his suspicions about the boy she was about to see, and he was winning more points by the day.

He's winning me over too easily.

Something that never happened—because she refused to allow it, was on guard about her feelings all the time. She had to protect herself and Mia. Except Nicolas seemed to be overriding all her barriers in one fell swoop.

How come that didn't send her running from the building? Thinking back to Friday night, a tingle of anticipation repeated itself. Excitement was possible if she opened up a little, relaxed and went with the new sensations Nicolas caused.

A loud metallic crash came from the sluice room, and some low mutterings.

'You all right in there, Liz?' Claire asked the nurse picking up a metal bowl from the floor.

'Having a brain fade moment,' Liz replied. 'Teach me to be daydreaming about the weekend and not focusing on what I'm meant to be doing.'

Eek. Better get ready to see Noah before my daydreams cause me to do something silly.

Within moments her room was crowded, her young patient looking bewildered and scared. His mother appeared defiant, but the fact she was here with her son said lots in her favour. 'Hello, I'm Claire, one of the doctors. Are you Mrs Robertson?' she asked the woman firmly gripping the lad's shoulder as Nicolas showed them in.

'That's me. Noah was playing around on the kitchen stool when he fell off and hit his face on the highchair. He says it's very sore and one eye has closed up.'

'Take a seat.' Claire closed the door and

moved to her desk. 'I'm going to touch your face, Noah, to find out if there are any broken bones under those bruises. Is that all right?'

'Yeah.'

'Sit up and speak nicely,' Mrs Robertson growled.

The boy shuffled his bottom on the chair.

'Look up at me, Noah.' Nicolas was right about older bruises under the red and purple swellings. She suspected he'd also got it right about the abuse. 'Tell me if I hurt you,' she added softly.

'He's tough,' the mother said.

When Claire felt along the cheekbone Noah winced and jerked sideways. 'That hurts there?' she asked.

'Lots.'

Sitting down, Claire typed some notes into Noah's file. It wasn't the first time he'd been to the Urgent Care medical centre with a fracture, which might make the conversation she was about to have more difficult.

'Mrs Robertson, I see Noah has other, older bruises on his face. Did he have another fall a few days ago?'

'Yes. He's clumsy like that.' The woman looked everywhere but at her.

'Did you take him to get medical help then?'

'No. He said it wasn't hurting too bad.'

Claire's finger was tapping her thigh as she asked, 'Are you sure he fell?' If anyone hit Mia she'd be after them like a crazed woman. 'It seems odd to have bruising in the same place, that's all.' That wasn't the half of it, but softly, softly was the only approach.

'I brought him here to get fixed, not to be questioned like I've done anything wrong. Come on, Noah. We're going home.'

'Wait, Mrs Robertson. Noah needs to have a facial X-ray because I believe there are broken bones in his cheeks. It's really important to find out so we can fix them without him suffering more pain. We don't want that, do we?'

'No, I suppose not. But what if they were broken the first time he was hurt?'

'Let's wait until we know if there are any fractures. If there are then I'll be referring Noah across to the hospital to see a paediatric orthopaedic surgeon. A child's bone doctor,' she explained as Mrs Robertson started to look confused.

Relief replaced the confusion. 'That's good.' She probably thought the questions about how Noah had sustained his injuries would go away when they saw a specialist. She was wrong, but Claire wasn't about to tell her so.

'First I would like to give Noah a thorough check-up.'

Nicolas immediately helped the boy onto the bed. 'Lie on your back, Noah. I'll lift your shirt so the doctor can see your chest. Okay?'

Noah stared at Nicolas as if debating whether to trust him. 'Yeah.'

'Got to make sure you're all good everywhere else,' Nicolas told him.

No internal swelling around his organs, Claire noted.

Nicolas helped Noah roll over onto his stomach, and his mouth tightened.

Three old bruises covered the boy's shoulders. Claire touched them lightly. 'Any pain here, Noah?'

The boy moved his head back and forth on the pillow.

Bet you hurt when those were inflicted.

'Can I look at your legs?'

Nicolas was already preparing him for further examination. She hadn't had to say anything but she did want Noah to hear her talking so as not to get too spooked. He already had enough to deal with and his mother wasn't saying a word.

Minutes later she sat down at her desk and filled in some notes. 'Mrs Robertson, Noah needs to go to radiology urgently.' It wasn't an urgent case but any time spent sitting in the waiting room would be risky. He might be taken away without any treatment at all.

The woman sat there, gripping her hands in her lap, keeping silent.

'You want him to be taken care of, don't you?' Reminding her of why she'd brought Noah here in the first place might ease the tension.

Her head dipped slowly. 'Yes,' she whispered.

'Noah, I'm getting you a wheelchair and taking you for a ride. What do you think?' Nicolas asked.

'Okay.'

Nicolas looked to Claire, sorrow in his eyes. 'Give me a moment to find Liz. She'll take over triage while I help Noah. I'll stay with him.' He understood what she was worried about.

'Thanks.' Empathy came to mind. Most men were empathetic around children. She knew that, but sometimes had to remind herself that it was true. Her father had never hurt her physically, but he'd broken her heart when he'd walked out of her life. Mia's had done the same, though she was only now starting to understand what she was missing out on.

I want a cuddle from my daddy. Those words hadn't left her. Worse, there was nothing she could do about them. It was as though Hank had never existed. Except whenever she looked at Mia she saw his wide open smile and enjoyment of most things that came her way.

Nicolas returned quickly, pushing a child's wheelchair. 'Let's go, buddy. Mum's coming too.'

'I'll see you soon, Noah,' Claire said. *You'll be under constant care so you can't be removed from the hospital until this is sorted.*

Claire's heart felt heavy. 'That poor little boy. Why doesn't his mother stand up for him?' she asked Nicolas when he returned half an hour later to say Noah had been admitted with fractured ribs and cheekbones.

'She's probably another victim. I saw a bruise on her upper arm when the sleeve of her tee-shirt shifted. She was quick to pull it down,' Nicolas said angrily. 'Some men don't deserve children.'

'Or wives,' Claire agreed, then instantly regretted saying that.

He glanced her way, as if to check her out.

'No, I've never been physically abused by anyone,' she added quickly.

'Glad to hear that.' Nicolas wasn't looking away though. Almost as if he could see right inside her and knew she had more to tell.

Which she had no intention of doing. Not

now, more than likely not ever. It was a sad, pathetic story that she'd come to terms with as an adult, accepting her mother couldn't change and that deep down she'd loved her daughter. That alone had kept Claire at home looking out for her until she'd suddenly packed up and headed to Perth. Her mother had loved deeply and never got over what she'd lost, even when inadvertently inflicting pain on her daughter.

No wonder I am afraid of loving too much, Claire thought. Not true. She loved Mia more than she'd once have believed possible. Did that mean she might one day love a man as much? On a positive day she'd say anything was possible. She'd loved Anthony with all she had. Look where that got her.

Nicolas refocused her with, 'There's another priority one patient for you. Twenty-four-year-old male, heart palpitations, high BP, light-headed. Fell at work. I've put him in a bed and attached the monitors.'

'Name?' She turned for the room where four beds were ready for patients who needed monitoring.

'Jason Maynard.' Nicolas stepped away, stopped and turned around. 'You agreed with me re that boy?'

'Yes, one hundred percent. I'll call the child therapist once I've seen Maynard.'

'Good.' His smile went straight to her belly, and made her feel warmer than she already was.

There was a bounce in her step as she went to her next patient. Anything was possible on a good day, and seeing Nicolas at work, being on the same wavelength when it came to a patient, went some way to making this one of the best. Almost as if she hadn't a care in the world.

At five-fifteen Claire walked into the child-care centre to the sound of tired children grizzling. Mia was pushing a plastic truck around the sandpit with Kent. 'Hi, you two. Have you had a good day?'

'Kent ate my sandwich, but I had his chocolate cookie because he didn't want it.'

'He's conning you already.' Nicolas spoke from the other side of the room. 'He loves those biscuits.'

So he was picking Kent up again. Made perfect sense since Evelyn hadn't come into the centre today. He had the makings of a good dad. The lad seemed to adore him, and they had a great rapport. How had he fooled Kent when he was Santa? His voice would've been familiar, surely?

'Kent's not saying anything,' Claire observed, unable to deny feeling happy to see Nicolas, despite having spent all day in the same building, bumping into each other, discussing patients, sharing a coffee break.

Nicolas laughed. 'All part of the plan, suck 'em in and make them think he's the best boy in the play centre.'

'Who did he learn that from? His father, or his father's mate?'

Was that what Nicolas had been doing to her at the barbecue? Sucking her in so she thought he was the best thing out? She might be a fool, but so far she hadn't seen any ill intent in his actions. So far she couldn't fault him. Her eyes were wide open, so when he wanted to be kind and supportive and made sure her glass and plate were full, there'd been no argument from her. She was ready for a little fun.

Air stuck in her throat. That was her usual relationship—a little fun before pulling the plug, no feelings involved or hurt. That mightn't be enough with this man. Not that she understood why. Or did she? At least she was being cautious. She'd sent him away on Friday night when he'd dropped her off. No coffee or a nightcap, nor a kiss, let alone sex. She'd suddenly gone coy on him. Which said more than just about anything else could. When she wanted sex with her date, she got on with it, nothing like she'd been around Nicolas. Not that they'd been on a date. Not officially, anyway.

'Who? Me?' He was still laughing.

'I thought so.' Claire was laughing right along with him—and feeling more comfortable with each passing second. Even after a day of working together and having no hiccups along the way. 'Right-o, Mia, time we headed home and put dinner on.'

'Nicolas, are we going now too?'

'We sure are, kiddo. Where's your bag?'

'On the peg.'

'Then get it, or you won't have a lunch box to fill for tomorrow.'

'You're not running around after him?' Claire watched the two kids race to the wall where their bags hung.

'What? Make him soft? No way. Evelyn would have something to say if I did that.'

'She's got you wound round her little finger.' They were all obviously close. The way Evelyn had befriended her made her think it wouldn't be too long before she was also part of that closeness.

'Only because I let her.' Nicolas took the bag Kent held out to him. 'She's been so good for Bodie, turned his life around when he was in a very bad place. I'd do anything to thank her for that.'

Claire's heart turned over. Most people had a history that had either made them strong or squashed them. Having understanding friends went a long way to helping. Nicolas was obviously one of those. The sort of man who'd be good to have on her side.

'I'm sure they've supported you too.'

'They believe in me, and I can't ask for anything more than that.' He turned away. 'Come on, kiddo. I've got water pipes to shift.'

He didn't think others believed in him? Who had hurt Nicolas for him to feel like that? He was so open and sincere. He worked hard for his patients, and the fact he also ran and operated a vineyard on his land said a lot about his determination and grit. He was very believable.

'See you tomorrow, Nicolas,' she called after him before rounding up Mia, who'd sat down with another girl who was dressing a doll in a wetsuit.

Nicolas waved over his shoulder. 'Sure will.'

Working together meant they'd see a lot of each other, but still a thrill of anticipation ran through Claire. Her job had become a whole lot more interesting and exciting. All because of a man who flipped her switches with a simple smile or a serious comment. For the first time since she could remember tomorrow and work couldn't come fast enough.

* * *

I let Claire see my vulnerability? When I'm taking things slowly. Nicolas kicked the tarmac with the tip of his sneaker as he waited for Kent to climb into the back of his four-wheel drive. He'd have sworn but certain little ears would pick up on the words faster than a lightning strike.

'I like Mia's mum,' Kent said as he clicked his seat belt in place.

'You like Mia,' he replied with a cheeky smile. 'You gave her your chocolate cookie.'

'Her lunch was nicer than my peanut butter sandwich. She had a cheese muffin and grapes.'

'Tell your mother, not me. I'm only here to give you a ride home,' he said with a laugh. Evelyn had enough to do without coming up with creative lunches for her son, who usually swapped them out with some other kid. But never his cookies. Just like *he* never said anything about needing to be believed in to anybody. Certainly not to a woman he'd only met a few days ago and was keen to get to know a whole lot better. Showed how much Claire was doing his head in.

Working with her hadn't helped. She was a competent, calm and skilled doctor. Not one patient he'd seen had left her office looking frazzled or upset, even when in pain or on their way to the emergency department next door. Apart from that young boy they'd believed had been abused. Turned out they were right. The boy was now having counselling, and, better still, the mother had admitted she needed help too. It had happened fast, partly because Claire had insisted. She'd been kind and discreet, and fiercely determined, and the woman had buckled fast. She'd even thanked Claire in a roundabout fashion. That family had a long way to go, but they'd taken the first step. He felt some pride in his small part. The medical staff were a team, a team he loved being involved in. More than that, he liked that Claire had joined the centre.

He liked Claire, full stop.

'Can I have an ice cream, Nicolas?'

'No, mate, you can't. It's nearly your dinnertime.'

Your mother would have my head on a tray if I stopped at the shop.

'Knew you'd say that.'

'Of course you did.' No harm in trying though. So, was he going to try to get know Claire better? It could mean risking his head and heart if he found more to like. Then there was her little girl to consider. Because they were a package. He already knew nothing

would ever come between those two. As it
should be. Any man Claire let into her life
had to be sincere and serious, otherwise she'd
be afraid of Mia being hurt. He got it. In buck-
etloads. And believed in it the same.

CHAPTER FOUR

'NICOLAS, THERE YOU ARE.' Mia rushed across to stop right in front of him and tipped her head far back to stare up at him. 'Mummy's here too.'

'I can see that,' he replied, tossing Claire a grin before looking around. 'Where's Kent?'

'Gone wees.'

'Then I'll have to wait for him, won't I? What have you been up to today, Missy?'

'Reading and learning to count some more numbers. You want to see what I did?'

'Of course I do.' He glanced over at Claire again.

She was laughing. 'You know better than to ask.'

He could spend hours listening to that sound. It made him spongy inside. Soft and happy. Glad they were getting along so well. 'I like hearing about their days. It's kind of cathartic after our busy ones.' He bent down to look at the paper sheet Mia held out to him, covered in colourful numbers on a ladder. 'You did that?'

'Yes. See—one, two three, four.' She poked at each number up to ten.

'Well done. You're very clever. You know that?'

'Yes.' Mia bounced away on her toes, arms wide as though trying to fly.

Unexpected softness wound through Nicolas as he turned to her mother, whose eyes were also filled with a similar softness that could only be love. A sudden need to envelop Claire in a hug, to feel her against him, filled him. This woman was undoing his resolve to go slowly. But he had to. For both their sakes. He felt she wouldn't take fast and loving before slow and caring. Could be she wasn't used to being loved so easily.

Was she like him in that she hadn't measured up to the standards of someone important and was now careful to look out for herself and Mia, to save them heartbreak? If that was so, then he'd be extra alert because he fully understood. But hey, because of that he had a career as a nurse which he loved, and was doing just fine with his vineyard. Sure, nothing like a top-notch surgeon, but there were times after visiting with his brother when he wondered how happy David truly was.

Claire rubbed her arm, her gaze still on her daughter, as she asked, 'What are you up to this weekend?'

Who? Me? 'More of the same. Checking the vines, mowing between the rows.' *Wondering what you're doing?* Ah, to hell with going slow. There was such a thing as a dawdle. 'Would you like to come out to my place tomorrow? Bring Mia to see Kent too.' For all he knew, Mia might've spent the first years of her life on a farm, and she wouldn't be interested.

'That's a lovely offer, but won't we be holding you up from those jobs?' There was a hesitancy about Claire that touched him. She didn't dive right in without checking where he stood.

'They'll keep. I deserve some down time. Have you organised—' he paused, looked to see how far away Mia was and relaxed '—the Christmas present?'

'All sorted. Got the last one in the shop. Guess what I'll be doing after a certain someone goes to bed on Christmas Eve? Hopefully I can work it out in time. More often than I like admitting, I mess up these things.'

'You have to put it together?' Unless… 'Here's an idea. How about I take the package home and do that for you, then deliver it to your house later on Christmas Eve?' He held his breath as he waited for Claire's answer.

'Why would you want an extra job when you're so busy?'

'Why not? I have hours to spare once the sun goes down.'

'The pieces of plastic are tiny.' She was mulling over the offer.

'What harm can it do? If I get stuck you can help me when I bring it around.'

'You're right. I'm being silly. Thank you. And if your offer to visit tomorrow still stands then I'd love to come out to your place.'

His lungs returned to normal. 'Done. I'll text the address. Come later in the afternoon and we can have dinner on the deck afterwards. Early enough for Mia,' he added. 'Kent will turn up at some stage. He's never far away. If he gets a hint that Mia's around I'm betting he'll be there with a bag of cookies.'

'Young love, eh? They're only four and look at them.'

The two kids were running around the play mat, laughing and shrieking. Maybe not young love, but they were happy. He felt much the same. Claire was coming to visit. What more could he want? Not answering that because there might be plenty. Every day he was open- ing up to the idea of engaging with her further.

Even to the point of letting go some of his reluctance over getting involved. Only a little, but that was a lot more than he'd managed in five years.

'When are we going, Mummy?' Mia was dancing from foot to foot, impatience plain on her face.

'Soon. Now quieten down, will you? I've got to finish making this brownie cake or we won't be going anywhere.' She'd decided to bake it for dessert since Nicolas was cooking dinner.

'I want to go now.'

'Go to your room and read a book or we won't go at all.'

Please do as you're told because I really want to see Nicolas.

Seeing his vineyard might show more about him, how he thought about the land and what was important to bring in a perfect harvest of grapes.

'But—'

'Now.'

Stamp, stamp, stamp went two little feet all the way down the hall.

Claire sighed, and then smiled. Being a single parent was not always easy, but the rewards were worth the hard moments. So she kept telling herself on the bad days. Mia was four.

She didn't dare think about the teenage years. Hopefully she wouldn't be on her own by then. It'd be great to have a man at her side and covering her back when the going got tough.

That man had to be someone she could trust with their hearts. Nothing like her father. Afraid to take the risk for so long, she was finally admitting she'd love to have that special person in her life. Whether Nicolas had started this, or the new life she'd begun here was the cause, she didn't know. Could be that she'd reached the point where there was only one way to go—forward, chasing those long-buried dreams to find happiness.

Her phone vibrated on the bench. Nicolas. He'd better not be cancelling. Disappointment hovered as she picked up. 'Hi.'

'Hey, Claire. Just checking that Mia eats barbecued chicken.'

Oh, wow. He was a softie. 'Chicken cooked any way is her favourite food. But you didn't have to go out of your way. She has to learn to accept whatever she's given. Except eggplant. She hates it and I accept that.'

'Not an eggplant in sight. Come out whenever you're ready. I've finished working for the day.'

'Is that Nicolas? We're coming now,' Mia yelled from the hall.

He laughed. 'Are you doing what you're told, Claire?'

'We're about an hour away from leaving here. I've got something in the oven.'

'That's okay. I've been mowing so I'll grab a shower before you get here.'

She wouldn't think about the picture those words conjured up. 'Okay.'

'I'd also better clear up the mess I've made in the kitchen. See you soon.' Nicolas was gone.

Her arms squeezed into her sides as she smiled to herself. As easily as that, Nicolas made her feel good about her parenting skills. He hadn't seen her in action around Mia often, yet knew how to make her feel proud. The few men she'd dated over the last four years hadn't been interested in Mia, other than to find a babysitter for her. That had hurt Claire and made her cagey. No wonder she thought Nicolas was something else. Special even. He'd certainly accepted she came as a package. He didn't ignore Mia.

'Mummy? When are we going?'

'Soon.' Right now would be great. Why hadn't she thought to make the brownie when she'd crawled out of bed that morning instead of doing the vacuuming? According to the timer, twenty-three minutes before she could take the cake out of the oven. Then it had to cool enough to be put on a plate and covered with a paper towel without steaming it into a gluey mess. Guess the added minutes would ramp up her anticipation and make for an even more enjoyable afternoon spent with Nicolas.

'I'm going to get ready. Are you wearing that top? Or do you want to put on the green one I bought last week?'

'I'm wearing this pink one. It's my favourite.'

Last week the pink and blue one was her favourite. Claire shook her head. She couldn't keep up. Where did her daughter get the fussiness from? *Probably me*, she decided after she'd tried on two pairs of jeans and two pairs of knee-length shorts and three tops. What did it matter what she wore? They all fitted nicely, suited her and highlighted her brown hair and tanned skin. Staring at the image in the mirror, she had to admit the sky-blue shirt with gold lines went perfectly with the navy shorts. Decision made. Now for sandals. That was a lot easier. Navy with gold edging, low heels that wouldn't get stuck in the ground if they went for a walk around the vineyard.

Brushing her hair away from her face, she sighed again. It had been a long time since she'd got in a tizz over what to wear on a date, and this was a visit to a vineyard, not a high-end restaurant, and she was enjoying every moment.

'Mummy, the timer's pinging. Can we go now?'

If only. 'Not so fast.' Placing the brownie on a wire rack, she stared at it, as if to cool it down quicker, and laughed at herself. This was crazy. 'Have you got a jersey and a pair of trousers to put on later if it gets cold?'

Mia's shoulders rose and fell. 'Yes, Mummy. You told me that before. They're in my bag at the front door. I put two books in the bag too.' She was way ahead of her mother.

'Good girl. I'll get a jersey for me.' Plus a bottle of wine. Yes, taking a bottle of wine to a vineyard owner's house might seem odd but she wouldn't go empty-handed. Apart from the brownie, that was. Which wasn't cooling down anywhere fast enough.

'It might need uncovering,' Claire said to Nicolas in his kitchen thirty minutes later. 'Mia was getting impatient.'

Not me. Oh, no.

She glanced at Nicolas and started laughing at the look in his warm eyes. 'All right, I admit it. I was ready to get on the road and didn't want to wait any longer.'

He laughed with her. 'It'll be yummy. Thank you, but you really didn't need to make anything. I've got it covered.'

'I'm sure you have, but it's how I am.' Her mother had instilled in her to always go to other people's home with some form of gift, be it baking, wine or a present. Not sure why she'd been so insistent, but Claire had taken it on board and never went empty-handed.

'Freshly baked brownie is a favourite.'

Polite or genuine, it didn't matter. Her feet itched to dance while the blood was racing round her body. She felt special.

'I'll remember that.'

He might become tired of brownie if she got to visit as often as she wanted to at the moment. Never mind, she made a mean carrot cake too. She looked around and stepped across to the bay window overlooking neat rows of grapevines. They went for ever, all facing north and south, and looked beautiful in the sunlight.

'Are those rows planted for optimum sun?'

'Yes.' Nicolas had come to stand beside her. 'If you've ever flown into Blenheim Airport you'll have noted the numerous vineyards going for miles and miles with the rows in the same direction.'

'I've only ever driven here, but I've heard

people talking about how impressive the view is from above.'

'It's endless. And expanding every season.'

'You don't worry there'll be too many vineyards and the prices for wine will start falling?'

'If I did that, I shouldn't be in the industry. It's a growing market at the moment, and that's what I focus on. I like your choice of Chardonnay, by the way. It's a good brand.'

That was a relief. 'I didn't know if you'd like it, but I do and that's my benchmark. I'm no expert.' How many people were? Surely it was about what you enjoyed?

'Experts are overrated in my book. It gets back to personal taste. Let's go outside and take a wander around.'

Good answers all round.

'Let's.' This was so ordinary it was fun. She didn't feel she had to be on her best behaviour, or act as if she was more than she wanted to be. 'How many acres have you got?'

'Forty, thirty of which are in vines, and I'm working on planting another five acres. It's been an interesting experience.' His voice resonated with pride and satisfaction.

'You enjoy it.'

'A lot.'

Nicolas checked to see that Mia was with

them. 'We'll walk around the sheds to the vines growing on that slope.' His arm brushed Claire's, sending sparks throughout her.

For a moment she thought he might take her hand, but instead he put some space between them. Why? It'd be wonderful strolling along holding hands. Could she reach for him? Take his hand? But this was a visit to see his place, not a hot date.

It is a date though. Isn't it?

Could she? Should she? The uncertainty was undoing her happiness.

'Watch out,' he said sharply, taking her hand to tug her sideways. 'There're a few sods of grass and soil between the house yard and the shed. I should've told you to wear boots or sneakers.' His hand was firmly wrapped around hers.

Happiness restored. She wasn't pulling away from the warmth and firmness of his hold. The buzz of adrenalin was heating her inside and out. He was too good to let go.

'I'll be more watchful.' *While making the most of this contact.*

His fingers started to let go. She tightened her grip. So did Nicolas.

They kept walking towards the sheds. A spontaneous smile broke out. Who'd have believed she could derive so much happiness from holding hands? Went to show how much she'd been missing out on. The move to Blenheim was opening her eyes to a future that held even more promise than work and being a mother. Opportunities to accept a man into her life.

It would be hard after her previous experiences to completely open up, but she was willing to give it a go. All because Nicolas tightened her belly and set her heart racing? Those counted for a lot. She couldn't imagine falling for a man who didn't make her heart sing and her body swoon. But there was so much more to Nicolas, like his kindness and genuineness, which were huge pluses in her book. So much more to find out about him before she'd be brave enough to trust her instincts.

Mia was skipping alongside Nicolas. When she tripped he reached for her but Mia pulled away. 'I don't need anyone to hold my hand.'

'That's good.' He looked slightly bemused.

Claire couldn't help herself. She laughed. 'She can be quite independent.'

He turned those stunning eyes on her and gave a half laugh. 'So I see. I'm not complaining. You all right?'

Her head dipped, then lifted. 'Absolutely.' He was a kind man. She was liking him even more. Well, that was what she wanted, wasn't it? Possibly. Probably. Try yes. 'Did you always want to be a nurse, or did that come about later when you'd been working somewhere else?'

His silence had her wishing she could retract her question. She didn't want to upset him. Though how she was to get to know him better if she didn't ask what seemed straightforward was beyond her.

His honed shoulders rose, dropped back in place. 'I wanted to be a surgeon.' Another shrug followed. 'Instead I quit school at sixteen and left home to go to Nelson, where I got work on a fishing trawler.'

She held onto the next question. He'd tell her if he wanted, and if he didn't she'd respect that, while itching to know the answer.

'No reason not to tell you. I was under a lot of pressure from my parents to go to med school and do as well, if not better, than my older brother.' Bitterness tainted his words. 'I'm as intelligent as David, as capable of qualifying as a medical specialist, and I would've done so if I wasn't continuously being compared to him.'

'That's hard. Plus unfair.'

'In the end it became too much, and I started to wonder who I was trying to please—my family or myself. Believe me, they weren't too happy about me being a fisherman. The funny thing is I loved it. I got a thrill being out on the water for weeks on end, beyond sight of land, and dealing with weather I had never experienced. I grew up fast.'

'Why did you stop?'

'Despite what I was doing on the water I still had a hankering to be involved in the medical world. By then I couldn't envisage spending the next ten or so years studying and being stuck inside endlessly, so nursing was the best option.'

'You balance that with this.' She waved her free hand around at the land surrounding them. It made perfect sense. He moved like an outdoors man, strong and confident, yet in the medical centre he was quieter, calm and gentle.

Nicolas swallowed hard, looked away, around at his property. 'You got it.' His fingers squeezed hers before he let go. 'Mia, want to feed the chooks?'

'Yes, please, Nicolas.'

There was more to his story. But the fact was, he'd shown her a vulnerable side and she respected that. Hell, she knew all about vulnerability. Her biggest being her gorgeous little girl chatting away to Nicolas as if he was her new best friend.

Her heart swelled for her child, and even for

the man showing Mia some weaned lambs. But watch out anyone who hurt Mia. They wouldn't stand a chance. She'd do anything to protect Mia from the hurt she'd grown up with. Anything.

Give up the chance of romance and love?

The crux of all her reasoning. If she ever settled down with a man, she'd be adding joy to Mia's life along with hers. A chill crossed her skin. Would she know she'd got it right or wrong before it was too late? She shivered. Getting involved was risky. For her. And her girl.

Watching Nicolas leading Mia to the chook pen with hungry hens chasing them, longing filled her, nearly dropped her on the ground. This was what she wanted—more than anything. Family. Love. Understanding and kindness. It might be here, hers for the taking if she was brave enough. But… Again her skin pricked. So many scary 'but's. Nicolas probably wasn't the slightest bit interested in a few innocuous dates. What did he really think of her? Another question she wouldn't be asking.

'Mummy, look. The chooks are going to be shut in for the night.'

Rubbing her arms, she joined them. 'Aren't they funny, the way they run?'

'I want one.'

'We haven't got a shed or lots of yard for one.' She refused to look at the laughter breaking out across Nicolas's face. It twisted her stomach and made her want to lean in and kiss him. Truly? Kiss Nicolas? Why not? Those lips were to die for.

Not in front of Mia.

Of course not. That was partly an excuse. So was the fact they didn't know each other well enough yet. Huh? She'd had flings where the kissing had started pretty damned fast, followed by what flings were made of. The fast follow-on wouldn't be enough with Nicolas, she suspected. Despite the multitude of doubts cramming her head, deep down her brain was telling her he was more than a fling. If she took the time to get closer and more intimate in ways other than physical, there might be a good chance of it turning into something special and lasting.

'Your mum's right. Chooks need somewhere to dig up worms.'

'Mummy eats chickens. I don't like that now.' Mia ate chicken like there was a famine about to happen, but now wasn't the time to point that out.

Nicolas raised an eyebrow. 'Dinner should be interesting,' he said in an aside.

* * *

Nicolas couldn't believe how much fun he was having letting Mia feed the chooks, with Claire at his side, chatting away about anything and everything as if she didn't have a worry in the world. Not once so far had there been any sign of reticence about being with him. He'd taken her hand without thinking too much about it, and when she didn't pull away it was as though he was floating over the ground.

Who'd have thought giving Claire a lift last week could've led to this? He would've met her at the function, but they might not necessarily have spent any time together. He'd probably still have been attracted to her, but it would've been harder to ask her out here.

'What can I do?' his daydream asked, looking very real and sexy in her fitted clothes and with those curls falling around her shoulders.

'Nothing. Everything's prepared. I just have to barbecue the chicken and we'll be ready.' They were eating early because of Mia. Claire had said to feed her first if he wanted, but this was fine. They'd still be together, sharing a meal and a glass of wine. He'd never been on a date that included children and he didn't mind Mia's presence at all. There'd be times when it would be preferable for just the two of them to be together, but at this early stage in the relationship—if that was what it was becoming—all was good.

At the moment Mia was on the deck chomping into crisps, which meant she could wait a bit for dinner.

'Bring your wine and we'll sit in the shade on the deck.'

Claire looked completely at ease as she went outside to sit down, crossing those slim legs and sipping her wine as if she'd been coming here often. 'This is so relaxing.'

Something he doubted she got to do often. 'Any time you want to get away from people or town, feel free to drop by. I can't guarantee I won't be busy, but make yourself at home. There's a back door key under that pot with the fern growing in it.' Would she do it? Claire appeared to like laying things out, not going in blindly.

'I'll bring more brownie.'

'Then you can stay for ever. That was yum.' He'd sneaked a piece as he was crumbing the chicken. He hadn't got away with it. A certain little miss had demanded some too, and for some inexplicable reason that made him feel accepted. He also felt a tad guilty about giving Mia brownie so close to dinner, as if he was trying to win her over, but Claire had merely shrugged and said it was all right this time. It was all a bit familyish. Kind of cool. Definitely comfortable. Something he hadn't known since he was a kid, before the pressure started to be applied. Did Claire come from a close family? 'Do you have any siblings?'

'Not a one.' Her smile dipped, then she seemed to gather a breath and plaster it back on. 'It was just me and my mother. Dad left when I was four.'

He'd been far better off than her then. Even the daily grind of trying to prove he was as good as David didn't take away the fact he'd had parents and a brother to spend time with. There were good memories of going fishing with his father, and Mum teaching him to drive.

'I'm sorry to hear that. Did you see much of him?'

She looked sideways at him, her eyes narrowed. Debating how much to say?

'It's all right. Don't feel you have to tell me anything that makes you uncomfortable.'

Slowly her eyes widened back to normal and the tension in her body eased off. 'I've never seen or heard from him since.'

'What? That's dreadful.' How could any man do that to his child? Or any woman, for that.

Insane, and selfish. And hurtful beyond understanding. 'How did you cope growing up?'

'Some would say I didn't. I played up badly for a few years, demanding to be noticed, accepted, and even loved. When that didn't work and I got kept back at school as punishment I did a complete about-face and became engrossed in study and keeping my distance from people.'

'What about your mother? Where was she in all this?' Surely she'd have gone out of her way to keep Claire happy and knowing she had at least one loyal parent.

'Pretty much in her own little world, pretending Dad was going to walk back in the front door any day and we'd all carry on as though nothing had happened. I only existed to be fed and clothed—the mechanical chores that didn't involve Mum's heart.' The level in her glass lowered quickly as she took a big mouthful. Then she shook her head in astonishment. 'I can't believe I just told you all that.'

She'd surprised him too. 'I'm glad you told me. It means a lot to know more about you.' How could any mother do that? Claire was so loving with Mia. Of course she would be after her childhood, but she *knew* how to be the loving, exceptional woman that she was.

Placing his glass on the floor, he reached for

her hand and squeezed. Doing that a lot today, he thought. Twice being a lot. 'You certainly don't let Mia think she's missing out on love. It's there in everything you do for and with her, even if you're growling about something she's done.'

'I hope so.' She sniffed, and looked down at their joined hands. 'I've worked hard to be the mother I never had.'

His heart squeezed tight for her and the love she'd missed out on. Life was so bloody unfair at times. Could she ever make up for what she'd lost? Could he help her? He'd like to. Heck. This was getting out of hand.

'Here.' He tugged a serviette from the set table beside him and passed it to her, his hand pausing to touch the back of hers. 'Wipe your eyes. Can't have little one seeing Mum crying.'

'Why are you so understanding? I'm not used to it.'

'Could that be because you don't usually admit other people's acceptance of who you are?'

Now her eyes widened in shock. 'How can you know that?'

'I didn't until you just confirmed it.' But he tended to be good at reading other people's pain. Had enough of his own to have learned to tread carefully and understand no one got away without some hurt in this world.

Claire scrubbed at her eyes with the serviette, and stared out beyond the deck.

Looking around for Mia, he saw her sitting inside on the couch with a small laptop on her knees. A furrow marred her forehead as she studied whatever was on the screen. She looked happy, not peeved about not being the centre of attention. Turning back to Claire, he smiled. It was time to lighten the atmosphere or the evening would be ruined.

'I'll put the chicken on the barbecue and get things underway.'

'Sounds good. Shall I get the salads out of the fridge?'

'Go for it.' *And while you're at it, throw me another of those beautiful smiles.*

'Nicolas?'

He turned around, and wham, right in the gut. A smile so darned beautiful he must've died and woken up in Utopia.

'Thanks. For everything.'

'Come here.' He had to do this. He had to, or bust apart. Winding his arms around Claire, he stepped back out of sight of Mia and leaned in, placing his mouth on hers. Feeling her soft lips under his, her warm waist under his hands, her breasts pressing into his chest. He closed his eyes, breathed her in, then kissed her. Kissed and kissed, until he had to come up for air. She tugged him back, reaching up on her toes to find his mouth, and returned the kisses as deeply, as intensely, engaging him completely.

When Claire slowly pulled back he lifted his head and locked his gaze with hers. 'Claire,' he whispered, and stopped, no words coming to his tongue. Or his mind. She'd blown him away with those kisses.

Running her fingers down his cheek, she smiled ever so slowly and tantalisingly. 'I didn't expect this.'

'Me either.' He'd hoped they might get to kiss before she left to go home, but those kisses went way beyond a goodnight kiss. 'I don't know what's happening between us, but I'd like to spend more time with you to find out. How does that make you feel?' Might as well be blunt. If she wasn't happy then best he knew now and not a couple of weeks and more scintillating kisses down the track.

'Interested. Keen. And still wary.'

'So am I. But nothing ventured, eh?'

'Agreed. Now, we'd better get on with dinner before a little someone finds us and asks questions I have no answers for. Yet.'

Yet. Hopefully he'd manage to help her find all the answers she needed—and him—

over the coming weeks. With a quick hug he stepped away and turned the barbecue grill on, before going to get the drumsticks and thighs he'd crumbed earlier. His day had gone from ordinary to fun to exciting. He couldn't wait for more.

CHAPTER FIVE

'CLAIRE, THERE'S A patient in the monitoring room requiring urgent attention. I think she should be in ED.'

Claire put aside her coffee and followed Nicolas out of the staffroom. A week had passed since she had been out to his place, and in that time they'd worked together two days. 'What've we got?'

'Josey Brown, thirty-one, fell off bike alongside Taylor River. Rapid heart rate, light head, bruising on the ribs. No history in her file of anything other than a fractured tibia four years ago, though that mightn't be up-to-date.'

'Why is she here and not ED already?'

'Her partner brought her in, and won't listen to Charlene telling her to go next door. The partner's not someone I'd argue with either.'

'I might be about to.' She stepped into the room and crossed to the only occupied bed, where another woman sat on a chair, looking ready to pounce. 'Hello, I'm Claire McAlpine, a doctor. Can you hear me, Josey?'

'Hmm.'

It was something, though not enough. 'I understand you came off your bike. Did something go wrong with your ride? Or did you have a medical incident that caused you to crash?'

'She wobbled after dodging a small rock and fell,' the partner answered, glaring at her. 'We've told the nurse all this.'

'I'd like to hear what Josey has to say,' Claire said in her firm, I'm-the-doctor tone. 'Josey?'

'Was light-headed. Rock in the way. Lost control.' Her speech was a little slurred and disconnected.

'Pain anywhere else?'

'No.'

'Any history of headaches, high blood pressure?'

The partner interrupted. 'What's with all these questions? Why aren't you examining Josey?'

'I'll get there a lot quicker if you let me do my job,' Claire replied, and noted a glint of interest in Nicolas's eyes. Didn't think she could be tough when required? He had a lot to learn. 'Josey, answer me.'

'No.'

'No history, or no you won't answer me?' Pedantic maybe, but necessary if she was to make an informed decision about the woman's condition.

'No history.'

'She's very fit.' The partner added her bit.

Fitness didn't give everyone a clean bill of health all the time. 'What about family history of high blood pressure or strokes?' She read the monitor, noted the raised blood pressure.

'My mum.'

Again her partner interrupted. 'Her mother had a fatal brain haemorrhage at the age of fifty.'

You knew that and didn't go to ED?

There was a possibility Josey could be following in her mother's footsteps. 'Right, this is what we're doing. Josey, I am transferring you to the emergency department, where they have more equipment to monitor you. They can also admit you to hospital, and call on a specialist.'

'Why can't you do that from here?'

'Because we're a private centre, and all our cases go through either ED or back to a patient's GP.'

'This is wasting time.'

Nicolas was reading the heart monitor and said, 'Josey's getting excellent care right now. Taking her through to the hospital department will up the ante.' He flicked Claire a look of *What the hell?* and said aloud, 'I've got this,' with a small smile aimed directly at her.

Even here that smile got to her, touched her and said she wasn't on her own. He was efficient and understanding. A top-notch nurse in all respects.

Returning his smile with a soft one of her own, she said, 'I'll fill in the details for ED.'

'Josey, you're going for a ride,' Nicolas said.

'I'm coming with you.' The other woman stood up abruptly.

'Of course you are. It's always best when someone else is with the patient and hears what the doctors have to say,' he replied.

Claire smiled to herself. He was as annoyed with the partner as she was and still being respectful. The woman was no doubt very worried about Josey, and it was coming out in a rude way, but Josey was the one who was ill and who needed all their attention and care. 'I'll check to see how you're getting on later, Josey.'

At her desk, Claire typed up the notes while ringing ED to inform them of her patient's problems. Next she clicked on the list of patients waiting to be seen.

'Samuel Crowe.' Her gaze fell on a small boy curled up in his mother's lap, and presumed he was the two-year-old she was looking for. 'Mrs Crowe?' Receiving a quick nod, she said, 'Bring your son through. I'm Claire McAlpine, your doctor this morning.'

'I'm Sharon. Sorry to bother you, but I'm worried. Sam's not breathing properly.'

'Let's lie him on the bed. And you're not bothering us. If your child is unwell never think you shouldn't bring him in for a check-up. It's far better to be safe than find out later there was something seriously wrong.'

'I know, but I worry a lot over the smallest things going wrong.'

She knew that feeling all too well. 'As any good mother does. Tell me what made you bring him in, Sharon.'

'He's been over-tired and grizzly, and then he started crying and breathing funny. I put him to bed early, and kept checking on him all night, thinking the breathing would get better, but it's no different this morning.' Her fingers were rubbing her son's arm.

Sam was red in the face and his breathing was laboured and there was a distinct whistling sound. Getting a stethoscope, Claire smiled at the little boy. 'Sam, I'm going to put this on your chest. It might feel a bit cold at first, but it won't tickle. Okay?'

He stared as she placed the chest piece on

his hot skin and, when he didn't react, she listened to his lungs with one ear and heard Sharon out with the other.

'Mummy?' The little guy's eyes had filled with fright.

'It's all right, love. This lady's going to make you better.'

No pressure. 'Sam, you're doing well. I can hear you breathe through this.' She held out the earpiece for him to see.

'Need a hand in here?' Nicolas had returned, and she hadn't noticed. Her Nicolas radar had failed.

'Sharon, this is Nicolas. He's a nurse. I'm going to get him to take Sam's temperature.'

'Hey, Sam, that's a cool shirt you've got on.' Nicolas grinned at the boy.

'Has Sam ever had breathing difficulties before?' she asked Sharon.

'Once or twice he's made funny wheezing noises but nothing like this.'

'This is an asthma attack. At the moment I don't know what brought it on. It could be an allergy or a viral infection. I'm going to prescribe an inhaler to start using immediately, and refer him back to your GP for ongoing tests to find the reason for this onset.'

'Temp is thirty-seven point seven,' Nicolas informed her.

'Slightly raised.' Filling in the prescription form on screen, Claire glanced at the cute little boy sitting up with Nicolas's help. His big eyes were fixed on the nurse, as if he had all the answers to his problems. Something she could understand, because he made her feel the same at times. 'Here you are. Take that to the pharmacy and get Sam started on the inhaler as soon as possible. You'll notice a difference quite quickly. If not, bring him straight back.'

'Hey, Sam, can I carry you out to the car?' Nicolas asked.

'Yes.'

'Thank you both. It's so worrying being a parent.' Sharon watched her son cling to Nicolas as they headed for the door.

He had a way with kids that was endearing, and something Claire trusted.

'I'm a mum, I know where you're coming from.'

'I hear doctors are far worse when it comes to their children needing medical help.' Finally there was a hint of a smile on Sharon's face.

'There's something in that. Take care, and go to your GP ASAP.'

'Yes, Doctor.' The smile improved, showing a lovely woman behind the worry for her son.

'Sharon's on the phone making an appointment already.' Nicolas stood in the doorway five minutes later. 'She was impressed with your calm approach.'

'Sam isn't my son. It's easier.'

Stepping into the room, he closed the door and leaned back against it. 'Would you like to go out for dinner tonight? I'm sure Michelle would be happy to babysit. She's always looking for extra money.'

So she couldn't use Mia as an excuse to say no. Did she want to? Nicolas's invitation had instantly made her glow on the inside. Going out for dinner wasn't rushing things between them. Instead it would give them time together away from here to relax and chat about anything and everything.

'I'd love to.'

He blinked. Hadn't expected her to accept so quickly? A wide smile lit up his face.

'Great. I'll make a booking. Want me to talk to Michelle?'

'I can do that.'

'I'll pick you up at six-thirty.' The door opened and he was gone, back to being a nurse, not her date for the night.

Grand. She was going on a date, dinner with the man who'd made her start changing her thinking about men and relationships almost before she'd learnt his name. Bring it on, said the buzz under her skin. Two dates without getting too deep too soon was new for her. Since she'd become a mother anyway.

Six-thirty. That would keep her moving. Pick up Mia, bath and feed her, have a shower and find the right dress to wear. Try not to get nervous. Work harder at not trying on every summer dress she owned before tossing them aside. Forget nervous. She was going with excited. Damn, but this move was turning out to be much more fun than she'd ever anticipated.

Picking up her phone, she texted Michelle.

'Hard to believe it's almost Christmas.' Claire pushed her dessert plate aside and leaned back in the chair in the restaurant. 'I could've sworn it was only a few months since last time.'

'You'd have been in Dunedin then.' Nicolas twirled his empty wine glass in his fingers. 'It's been a busy year for you, packing up and moving and starting a new job.'

'Most of that's happened in the last few months. Maybe that's why the year seems to have flown, it's all been about the second half. Come to think of it, the first six months were uninteresting.' Mostly packing up her mother's house and possessions, selling what she hadn't wanted to take with her, which turned out to be just about everything.

'Who did you spend Christmas with last year?'

'A friend and her family.' Thank goodness for Cheryl or it would've been a quiet day for two. Mia at least had other kids to unwrap presents and play with. 'My mother never did like celebrating Christmas or birthdays.'

'I'm sorry to hear that. It can't have been easy,' Nicolas said.

The night before her mother was due to fly to Australia had been the first and only time she'd ever told Claire the words she'd waited a lifetime to hear. Claire had been dozing when she sensed her mother approach and sit on the edge of her bed. It was unusual for her mother to come so near, let alone run her hand down Claire's arm before saying for the first time ever, 'I love you, Claire. I always have. I'm so proud of you and everything you've achieved, including Mia.' After a few silent minutes, she'd added, 'Don't make the same mistakes with your life I did with mine.' Then she'd left the room, leaving Claire gobsmacked. And finally at ease with her mother. She was loved, and that was all she'd ever wanted.

Next morning, when Claire had returned from dropping her mother off at the airport, she'd found the silver ring that had been her grandmother's and which her mother always wore on her bedside table. Claire had worn it ever since, accepting it as her mother's way of backing what she'd said the night before.

Now her mother's words resonated in her head. A bit like Mia's when she was sitting on Santa's knee, they came back to haunt her at the most inconvenient moments.

'That's Mum.' Phone calls were rare and stilted, as though she regretted what she'd said. But the words remained in Claire's heart.

'It's hard when people won't share their thoughts and emotions.' Nicolas was staring at the table as he spoke.

'Some people tend to show it in how they help each other, whether it's getting the car running when the engine died, or being there when their world is turning upside down.' Not when leaving their daughter behind, though. Bet Nicolas was always there when needed, by a friend, or his family, despite their expectations of him driving a wedge between them all. So far, it was hard to fault him over anything, but it would come. No one was perfect, and if she expected him to be she'd be in for a big disappointment.

'Where did you get to be so wise?' He was smiling now, looking at her and not the table.

'It must've rubbed off someone when I was standing in a crowded bus one day.' It paid to lighten the atmosphere further or she might get too deep about why she and her mother didn't spend much time together. Strange how right now she'd love to open up and talk about how her mother had kept her emotions locked down. However, while they were getting closer, she was still cautious about what made her hesitant. Her vulnerability was not for show.

'Which bus? I could do with gaining some wisdom over certain matters going on in my life.' He was still smiling so they couldn't be bad issues. Or was he good at hiding his true feelings? He *was* always friendly and cheerful.

Unless a patient's partner got stroppy about how the treatment was being arranged, Claire remembered. 'I'll buy you a ticket for Christmas.'

'Can't wait. Shall I pick up the kitchen set when I take you home?'

She still felt a little awkward about Nicolas taking over making the present for her, but it would save a lot of trouble.

'Good idea. It's locked in the boot of my car. I couldn't stow it anywhere in the house as Mia has a tendency to go looking through cupboards for no other reason than she wants to. Finding the kitchen box set would ruin the magical Christmas moment. It'll only be another year, maybe two, before the truth's out about Santa, and I want to keep her young and naïve for as long as possible.'

'Not for too long, or then you'll be wishing she'd hurry and grow up and get some sense in her head. Believe me, I've seen it all with Evelyn and Michelle.' Nicolas laughed. 'Evelyn worried about introducing another man into Michelle's life but Bodie handled it so well they got on well from day one. Evelyn was divorced and her ex moved away, but he does have Michelle to stay every school holidays. Then along came Kent, and Michelle's still as much a part of the family as she always was.' There was an intensity in Nicolas's face now, as though he was wondering how she would feel in the same situation.

Answer? Mia had to be happy with the man Claire settled down with. The man in front of her? Too soon to know, or to be thinking along those lines. Except he made her feel. Feel as in being alive and happy and excited.

'Sounds ideal. That's what I want for Mia if I find someone to share my life with.' Not saying anything else. That was too much.

'As you should. I can't imagine a man, or a woman come to that, not accepting their partner's children as part of the deal. There's so much to gain, and nothing to lose.'

Good answer.

'I agree. But then I'm on the other side of the picture.'

'Can I take your plates?' the waitress asked, reminding Claire they weren't alone.

'Thank you.' She moved her dish to the edge of the table.

'Is there anything else you'd like? Coffee, tea? Another wine?'

'Claire?' Nicolas raised one eyebrow.

'Not for me. Coffee would keep me awake half the night. But you go ahead.'

'No, think we'll hit the road.'

Walking out to his four-wheel drive, Nicolas slipped his hand around hers, and she leaned a little closer. 'I haven't enjoyed myself so much for a long time.' Since Saturday at his place.

'Funny you should say that because I feel the same.'

That had to be good. They were on the same page. But he must've been dating other women. He was good-looking, and had more good attributes other than the physical ones.

'You can't have been single for too long.'

'Depends what you mean by single. I've been out with a few women, but there's been nothing serious going on for years.'

Why? A back story that made him wary? Or

too busy with his work and vineyard to expend his leftover energy?

'I find that hard to believe.'

'Back at you.'

She hadn't told him how sparse her dating life had been. Was she so obvious? Probably if the way she got excited over being asked out to dinner was an indicator.

'Relax. I can't see you going overboard with anyone who didn't fit in with your position as a single mum.'

'I was in a bit of a rut before I moved here. Shifting homes, jobs and towns seems to have given me a boost. Getting out and about is fun, meeting new people and working in a different environment makes me feel pleased about the changes.'

'I'm glad you shifted this way.' They'd reached his four-wheel drive and he took her in his arms, gazed into her eyes. 'Very glad.' Leaning closer, his eyes still locked with hers, he said softly, 'Claire, thank you for coming out with me tonight.'

'More than glad I did.' *Please kiss me.* Would he? Wouldn't he? 'Nicolas?'

'Ahh, Claire.' Pulling her even closer, he leaned down to place his mouth on hers. Paused as though waiting for permission to continue.

Pressing her lips against his, she slipped her arms around his waist and relaxed into him.

Nicolas's mouth claimed hers as he began kissing her without restraint.

Desire swamped her, turning her body soft and limp, and stalled every thought, gave credit only to the sensations rolling throughout her. When Nicolas slipped his tongue between her lips, she held him tight. He knew what he was doing, and she had to have more. Holding that gorgeous, muscular body, she pressed more firmly against his mouth, kissed back as if she had no intention of ever stopping. Which she didn't.

Only one of them had to be sensible. Eventually. Soon.

Nicolas lifted his mouth from hers slowly, tantalisingly. 'We'd better go before the staff come out and send us packing like a couple of teenagers.'

Really? When she was having so much fun, and getting all wound up with desire. He was probably right, but at the moment she didn't want right, she wanted enjoyment. The heat of the moment had slain all her doubts and worries about getting involved.

She straightened, brushed her hands down the front of her dress. *Not wise to continue, Claire.* It was risky diving in when she wasn't certain Nicolas was the man for her. This was nothing like a quick fling. If she was to be intimate with him it had to be for the right reasons, and to be reciprocated. There'd be repercussions if they got it wrong. For her, and for Mia. Possibly for Nicolas, considering how seriously he seemed to be taking this.

'Take me home,' she said on a long sigh. Then hoped he didn't think that was an invitation to stay over. No, he was giving Michelle a lift back to her place. Damn it. All the same, she felt some relief that the rest of the evening was sorted.

Her head was all over the place. She wanted Nicolas, and everything he had to offer. She needed to be careful and look out for herself. *Steady does it.* Except, for once, steady wasn't in her vocabulary. She laughed, and felt free in an unusual way, all because of Nicolas. While that was a warning in itself, she carried on smiling. She was happy.

As Nicolas pulled out onto the road, she said, 'Let's go somewhere at the weekend. Take Mia to the beach and have a picnic.' Then she held her breath. He might not want to follow up on tonight. But how could he not when he'd just kissed her as if his life depended on it?

'You're on.'

She slumped into the seat, still smiling. 'I'll bring the picnic.'

'I'll bring the towels,' he joked.

'Sounds like fun.' And some.

What happened back there? Nicolas asked himself as he drove to Claire's house. She blew his socks off. With a kiss. A few kisses. Then minutes ago she'd suggested going out at the weekend, which had to be good, had to mean she wanted more kisses. Thank goodness, because he sure as anything needed more.

Easy does it. There'd be a little girl with them so kissing was out. They'd find a way round that. Mia would get tired at the beach with swimming and building sandcastles, then they'd head home. Wouldn't she? Fingers crossed she did.

Pulling into Claire's drive, he turned the ignition off and turned to her. Ran a finger over her arm, tried to ignore the heat that was rushing up *his* arm and deep inside. But he couldn't, so, unclicking their seat belts, he reached for her and hugged her tight. Then found her lips and began kissing her. Sinking into the heat filling his body, he knew wonder, and happiness. Something else was stirring through him too. A sense of homecoming, of having found someone who cared about what he felt.

His head shook abruptly to banish that thought. Might be reading too much into a few kisses.

'Nicolas?'

He'd broken their kiss. But that might be for the best after those thoughts. He wasn't ready for deep and committed. Would he ever be? He'd like to think so. He did want a future that included a loving and lovable wife, and a family. Over time the hurt of the past had gone, leaving him hollowed out, but since meeting Claire he was starting to feel whole again.

'Should I be going inside?'

No, damn it. 'I'm sorry. I was having a moment, that's all.' That was enough. His mouth covered hers before she could ask why. This was not the time to talk about his past. Not that he had a clue what constituted the *right* time. But now, kissing this amazing woman was all he wanted, and needed.

He kissed deeper, stroking Claire's mouth with his tongue, blotting out everything but the taste of her, the feel of her butt under his hands. It felt as if they were in their own space, where nothing could interrupt them. Except eventually they had to get out of the four-wheel drive and walk up to the house, where his friends' daughter waited to be driven home. His arms held Claire tighter, not wanting to let her go.

His lips brushed her cheek. 'I've had the best time.' He'd been going to say *night*, but there were plenty of hours left, hours that he wasn't getting to spend with her. Unless… No. He didn't think she'd be inviting him to come back after dropping off the babysitter. Claire kissed him like there was no tomorrow, but he already knew her better than that. She'd be cautious about inviting him to stay the night. She wouldn't want Mia waking up and finding him in her mother's bed when they weren't in a serious relationship.

'I'd better go in.' Her voice was clouded with disappointment.

At least that was his interpretation, but he might be looking for something that wasn't there. 'Fair enough.'

He held her hand as they walked to the door, only dropping it when she stepped inside. Following her, he had to laugh when he saw Michelle curled up on the couch watching something on her laptop. 'I bet you wouldn't hear Mia if she called out.'

Michelle jumped in shock. 'Hello. How long have you two been standing there?'

'Don't listen to him. We just arrived.'

Claire's face had a red tint going on. A result of those kisses?

'Come on. You can finish watching whatever's so enthralling you didn't hear us come in when you get home.' Now he sounded like a father. Glancing at Claire, he wondered what lay ahead for them. She was right. It was time to head home. Lots to think about before he got too serious about a relationship with this woman. He didn't want to hurt Claire, or be hurt in the process.

Valerie had thought he wasn't good enough, and found another man while she was still with him. His family believed he hadn't done what he was capable of, thereby letting them down. He hadn't let himself down though. He didn't regret his career choices. Not often anyway. But what if he let Claire down? What if she walked away without looking over her shoulder? Found another man to flaunt in his face?

What if he didn't take a chance and never found love? That would almost be worse than falling in love and losing her later.

'Nicolas, are you still on for the picnic?' Concern radiated out at him from those beautiful brown eyes locked on him.

'Try stopping me. I'll talk to you later and we can arrange times.' He wasn't working at the medical centre tomorrow. It was a vineyard work day. Fresh air and no hassles with difficult patients. No sensuous woman distracting him at every turn.

He brushed a light kiss on her cheek. 'Take care, and thanks again for a great night out.'

'You too.' Her eyes lit up. 'Talk soon.'

Now there was a thought.

At home, Nicolas slipped between the sheets and pressed Claire's number on his phone. 'Hey, you tucked up yet?' Blanking that image from his mind took effort, mostly a failure at that.

'Been here for ten minutes.' Her voice sounded husky.

Which stirred him, made him hard. What was she wearing? He opened his mouth. Closed it again. Then, 'You looked stunning in that dress tonight.' She'd worn a fitted turquoise number that showed every curve to perfection. No wonder he'd kissed her as if all his Christmases had come at once. He was getting harder thinking about it.

'Thought I might've gone over the top, but I love getting dressed up.'

It didn't happen often—was that what she was saying?

'Then wear something fancy to the beach for our picnic.' He'd never be able to stand up

or play games on the beach with Mia. He'd
be rock-hard. Already was. Phone sex would
help. Most likely kill the relationship for ever
if he suggested it. Of course he wouldn't. He
wasn't that stupid. Close, but not so close he'd
finish something that every day was growing into a special connection he hadn't known
since Valerie.

She giggled like a kid. 'I'll wear something
appropriate for swimming.'

*Oh, great. That'll cause just as much trou-
ble if she wears a bikini.* He could already
picture that lithe body covered in little more
than handkerchiefs. Did she have a wetsuit by
any chance?

'You do that.' Go to the charity shop and buy
a swimsuit his grandmother would've worn.
No, that wouldn't work. He'd seen photos of
his grandmother in her twenties, sunbathing
on the beach in a bikini. Only saying bikinis
were the thing even back then.

Claire cleared her throat. Was he getting to
her as much as she did him? He hoped so.

'I might see if Kent wants to join us on Saturday. He and Mia could play together.'

'Good idea.' They could lie in the sun and
talk, or... Nothing else. Two children would
be a bucket of cold water when he got too interested in Claire. This dating a woman with a

child was different. It came with handbrakes. Not that he was worried. Mia was fine and he had no issues with her being around. They wouldn't be going to the beach in the first place if not for her. But it did mean being aware he and Claire weren't alone when he felt frisky. Or just wanted to kiss her.

Which brought him right back to those decimating kisses they'd shared earlier. They were heating his body in all sorts of ways he didn't need if he was going to get any sleep tonight.

'I'd better grab some shut-eye. Sleep tight. See you on Saturday.' He finished the call before she said anything else in that sexy voice that'd screw with his head.

CHAPTER SIX

'CLAIRE, WOULD YOU and Mia like to join us for Christmas Day?' Evelyn asked during their snatched tea break at the medical centre the next day. 'I should've asked earlier. It's not a lot of notice, I know. Nicolas will be there too,' she added.

For a carrot, it wasn't bad, Claire thought.

'We'd love to.' It was as simple as that. Her new friends were fun to be with. Nicolas was more than a friend, but not yet a serious contender for the rest of her life. Getting closer by the day though.

'Come for breakfast, which is usually around nine, followed by a late and large Christmas lunch.'

'What can I bring? And don't say nothing. I've made a Christmas cake, which I have yet to ice.' It was a recipe handed down from one generation to the next on her mother's side, and absolutely delicious. She'd made it out of habit, thinking she'd bring it into work for everyone to enjoy.

'Bring that, please. I haven't made one this year. Actually I never make one.' Evelyn grinned. 'Not my thing.'

'What else?' She wasn't going empty-handed, which in her book meant more than a cake. 'I can get a salmon if you like.'

'Done.'

Claire sipped her tea and waited. She knew this woman well enough to know there was more to come and it wouldn't be about Christmas. Usually she'd dive straight in to bring up some uninteresting topic to cut Evelyn off but she didn't feel the need today. She was open to people knowing Nicolas was a part of her life and talking about weekend plans. Very different for her. It brought a sense of relief, as though a load had been lifted.

'So how is it going with Nicolas? You must be getting on well to be going on a picnic and taking my boy.'

See? Got that right. 'He's great.' At a lot of things.

'Come on. That can't be all.'

Claire ran two fingers across her mouth. 'My lips are sealed.'

'So are Nicolas's. Which tells me more than you realise. He's not a blabbermouth but he usually drops a few hints when he's been out with someone. Mind you, I haven't known him to date anyone quite like you.' When Claire lifted an eyebrow, she continued. 'He's taking his time, as if he really wants to get to know you well.'

'Much the same as I'm doing,' she admitted. 'I'm scared of making similar mistakes to past ones. Not that I see Nicolas as the type to hurt me.' Been wrong before though, so the closer she got to Nicolas the more afraid of commitment she became.

'There's a lot at stake. I get that, and I suspect Nicolas does too. Be aware he's very loyal to those he cares about. He's had his knocks, and won't be leaping in like there's no tomorrow.' Evelyn stood to rinse her cup. 'That's all I'm saying, apart from I'm glad you're getting along. I'd like to see him settled. He deserves it, and I think the same might apply to you.'

'It is the first time I've felt so hopeful. And happy,' she added on a deep breath, unusually fine talking to Evelyn about this. 'Thanks for inviting us to Christmas.' It was shaping up to be another great day.

What would the New Year bring? More magic? In the form of Nicolas? For the first time since she'd been with Anthony, she was looking forward, not backwards. Hank didn't count. He should be around for Mia, not her. New Year was supposed to bring new promises. Would next year come with all she suddenly wanted? What she was prepared to believe in because everything felt possible these days. Love, more family, happiness, trust, to name a few of her wishes.

New Year. A new life. Bring it all on.

The happiness factor was still there the next afternoon as she sat on the beach watching Mia and her little friend running in and out of the water with Nicolas chasing them, arms spread like a plane. He was as much a kid at heart as the two he was playing with.

'I'll be tucking you all in early if you keep this up.'

'Really?' he said, laughing. 'Does that come with a goodnight kiss?'

She'd walked into that one. 'Depends on how well-behaved you are.'

'That means I'll be out of luck, I guess.' He dropped onto the beach towel beside her and reached for a bottle of water in the cooler. 'They're energetic little blighters, aren't they?'

'What? You can't keep up?' She nudged a honed arm with her elbow.

'No comment.' Stretching out on his side, his head in his hand, he watched as she flicked her gaze between him and the kids, who were building a sandcastle nearly as high as Mia. 'How about you spend the evening at my place? I can rustle up a barbecue and the kids can catch a video. We could watch the sunset from the deck.'

He pressed the right buttons. It sounded like the perfect end to a wonderful afternoon. 'You're on. Drop me at my place first and I'll have a shower, make a salad and drive to your place so you don't have to take us home later.'

A hint of disappointment flashed across his face, before being replaced with a lopsided smile. 'If that's what you want. I can take Mia home with Kent. He can stay for a while if his parents agree. They might even join us.'

Touching his hand, she said softly, 'Thanks.'

Turning his hand over, he wrapped his fingers around hers. 'It's all right. I think I get it. Slowly does it. Part of me is on the same page, but then there are times I just want to leap in and see what happens.'

She opened her mouth to reply, but he held his hand up, palm out.

'We agreed the other night to go easy, and nothing's changed. Not much, anyway.'

'Meaning?' Had she done something wrong? Read him wrong?

'You kiss like the devil.'

Laughter burst through her concern. 'Same back at you.'

'Phew. I hate coming second.'

'Why does that not surprise me?' Leaning in, she placed a teasing kiss on his lips.

The next moment she was flat on her back with Nicolas on his elbows looking down at her with his eyes shining. 'You're not getting away with that, Claire McAlpine.'

'Careful, kids present,' she warned as she choked with laughter.

'They're busy.' His mouth claimed hers, and his tongue slid inside.

Her world went still. Everything about her focused on the sensations swamping her, driving her crazy with need. Slowly she breathed deep, smelt the salt and sun on his skin. Damn, she was gone. He had her in the palm of his hand.

Then he stopped, lifting his head and glancing around. Sitting up, he stared down the beach. 'They're heading this way.'

'Well timed,' she muttered through the desire pushing at her inside and everywhere.

'Call it luck. I was very distracted, yet knew I had to stop.'

Just as well, or she'd have lost all reason and given in to the bone-melting sensations filling her everywhere.

'I hate that you're right,' she admitted. Probably shouldn't be telling Nicolas how she felt, but he was being open and she wanted any relationship they might have to be open and honest.

'So do I,' he said ruefully. 'Only on this occasion,' he added with a shrug. 'Hey, guys, ready to go home?'

'No.'

'Do we have to?'

'We could stop for burgers and chips on the way,' he tempted.

'Yes!' Kent leapt into the air. 'My favourite dinner.'

'Can we, Mummy?' Mia asked. It would be a treat for her.

'Of course we can.' Though it was only five o'clock, not her dinner hour by a long time.

'I thought I'd cook something for you and me later, unless you're into burgers?' Nicolas asked.

'I don't mind a quick take-out occasionally when I can't be bothered preparing a meal, but honestly, right now it doesn't sound appealing.'

'Good answer. Right, guys, let's pick up our gear and hit the road.' He was folding his towel to put in the bag. 'Kent, you've left your sandals down by the water.'

'So?'

'So do you want a burger and chips?'

The boy trotted away in an instant.

'You'll make a great dad,' Claire said, laughing. 'You know which buttons to push.'

'The ones my parents used,' he replied with a grin.

'Mia, where's your bucket and spade?' she asked.

'Behind you, Mummy. They're wet and sandy. Too yukky to go in the bag.'

'Rinse them in the sea. I'll come with you.' To create a space between her and that seductive grin. Nicolas had a way about him that drew her in without any thought about where it might lead, and the more time they spent together the more she was concerned about where she was heading. He was turning out to be everything she wanted in a lifelong partner. Steady, kind, loving, and capable of turning her on in a blink. Almost as if she could leap in and take a chance. Trust Nicolas and her instincts. Mia sprang to mind, and her breath stalled. If Nicolas wasn't for ever then Mia would face rejection, which didn't just hurt. It stayed with a person for ever.

Glancing over her shoulder, she felt her stomach tighten when she saw him watching her with a similar longing in his expression. Impossible to ignore. Trouble was brewing.

'Good trouble, me thinks,' she whispered. 'Or hopes.' To go with it, or not? He'd invited her to join him for dinner, and they'd no doubt share a drink on his deck, and a moment or two without children interrupting. Go with it. There could be lots to gain. Her smile spread from ear to ear. She liked it.

'Comfy?' Nicolas asked Claire as he settled into a cane chair on his deck.

'Couldn't be better,' she acknowledged before sipping her wine.

Dinner had been a success and now they were having a second small drink to finish the day with. 'Give Mia another five minutes and I reckon she'll be sound asleep. Her head keeps nodding forward and she's slumped sideways over the cushions.' The little cutie hadn't even heard him say goodnight quietly, she was so close to being out to it.

'It's been a big day for her, playing for hours on the beach and swimming, then more playing with Kent here. Thank you for letting him join her.'

'No problem. It makes it easier for you, and fun for the kids. I think Evelyn and Bodie were grabbing the opportunity for some adult time.' Lucky buggers, he thought, and laughed at himself for cutting his own chances of adult time by having the kids here. But where Claire went, so did Mia. Most of the time. Today had felt like they were a family, and he'd loved every moment. He'd invite Claire out on another date, adults only.

'Who'd believe it's Christmas next week? The year has flown past.' Especially in the weeks since Claire came into his life.

'Did Evelyn mention we're coming out to their place for the day?'

'She did.' He paused as an idea struck. Nicolas drew a breath. Did he put it out there?

Claire hadn't finished. 'It's going to be a great day, being with others. Hopefully young lady will be so busy she won't remember what she asked you for and raising the point about a certain man's hug. I have no answer for her.' Claire's voice was wobbly, as if she was about to cry. 'Not one I'm ready to tell her yet. Not until she's older and hopefully able to understand a little. If I recognise that time and don't wait too long so it comes back to bite me on the backside. I'm sure you'd hug her if she asked, but that's putting a lot on you and could raise her expectations.'

Expectations Claire obviously wasn't ready for. Not sure if he was either. Reaching for her hand, he felt the shivers and held tight.

'You're a good mum. You understand your

daughter and I can't see you mucking this up. And, for the record, I would hug Mia any time she asked. I also see where you're coming from. None of it is easy.' To hell with it. He wanted to be there for her, to support her, and enjoy her company as often as possible. 'What would you say to you and Mia spending the night here? I have two spare rooms,' he added hastily, in case she was getting the wrong idea.

Not that he wouldn't mind sharing his bed with Claire, but he didn't know if she was ready for such intimacy. Or if she'd ever be. Though she'd been fast to kiss him back the other night, so he might be overthinking her reactions. Fast and mind-blowing. Yeah, he still felt the heat pinging through his blood now. Would he ever be the same again? It was one thing to have sex with a lovely-looking woman he liked, quite another to be intimate with a woman beautiful on the inside and out.

Suddenly he realised how quiet Claire had gone. 'It's all right. You can say no and I won't get upset about it.' Disappointed and sorry, but not cross.

Her fingers squeezed his, reminding him they were still holding hands, so not everything was off the table after his suggestion.

'I like the idea. As long as you're prepared for an early rising.'

His heart pounded as he replied. 'I'm used to getting up with the sun, so no surprises there. It might be you struggling to wake up, but I can remedy that with coffee or tea.' The pounding was still going on. He'd end up with sore ribs if it didn't slow soon. Claire was going to stay the night here next week. Maybe in the spare room, but definitely under his roof. It had to be a good sign of things to come.

'Tea that early in the day?' She withdrew her hand and clasped hers together on her lap, staring beyond the deck.

'Having second thoughts?' Better not be, because he was really happy about this, and the idea of her acceptance being retracted tightened his gut.

Twisting around, she faced him full-on. 'None at all. I admit to feeling a little cautious though. Every day we seem to move another step closer to each other, and that excites me. Until I stop and wonder what I'm doing.'

Instead of slowing, the pounding got harder. What was she about to say? Did she need some encouragement to see things his way? Or some time to think it through?

'Am I rushing you?' He'd put his hand up and take the blame, though in reality Claire was winding him up so fast and tight she had him in the palm of her hand.

'No more than I am. It's not something I'm used to.' She nibbled her bottom lip. 'I'm out of practice when it comes to relationships. Mia was the result of a short fling, not a long-term involvement.'

She'd said something about that the other day, and he'd been very surprised. She was so lovely that he'd have thought men would've been lining up to get her attention. That might mean she had reason to be ultra-cautious and therefore he'd made great inroads. Or he could be making it all up to justify the fact he cared one hell of a lot about her, and that was growing by the day.

'We could gain experience together. I like you a lot, Claire, and I don't want to walk away. Certainly not before I've given it everything I've got. I get that you're hesitant due to your past. I too have insecurities when it comes to trusting someone to accept me for who I am, and not who I should be. I was married once. She left me for another man and a job in another town when I believed we were trying to have a family.'

He stopped. No more words to put out there. He'd spilled his heart far too easily. Kind of said how much she was coming to mean to him. He wanted her to know he wasn't playing with her emotions, and that he had issues to work through as well. But it was hard. He didn't need Claire feeling sorry for him. Support and understanding was enough.

Claire's head dipped in agreement. 'That's lousy, Nicolas. Now I can begin to understand your issues with trust. The thing is, we're not twenty years old and full of expectations that everything love-wise will be a picnic.' She smiled. 'We've had one of those and it was wonderful.' Then the smile dipped. 'I wasn't making fun of it, I promise. I haven't had so much pleasure doing something so ordinary in a long time. That's because you were with me, with us.'

Us. Yes, Mia was a part of the picture, something that didn't bother him at all. He'd never known Claire as a solo act. Being a mother was part of who she was, and he had no problem with that. Nor with being a father to her daughter if they got that far.

'You couldn't have said it better. Thank you.'

'So, we're coming to stay here on Christmas Eve. I haven't had a fun Christmas for a while. Spending a whole day with you, and Evelyn, Bodie and Kent sounds wonderful. I can't wait.'

His muscles loosened as her words struck.

Claire was happy to be with him, and to stay the night. In one bedroom or another, he added optimistically. Might as well hope for the best, and not dwell on the negative.

'I'll have to get a tree and buy some decorations.' None in this house. There'd never been any need. It wasn't as if he'd put a present under it for himself.

Claire glanced inside. 'Mia's out for the count.'

He turned for a look. The wee girl was sprawled over the cushions, her eyes shut, and one hand touching Toby's head where he lay beside the couch. 'She fought it for a long time.'

'Nicolas,' Claire said softly.

He turned back to her. His breath caught in his throat. Her lovely face was so close he could see golden flecks in her eyes. And longing. For him. Yes, he knew it was for him. Because he felt the same for Claire. Longing, and tenderness, and a sense of love.

'Claire,' he whispered.

Leaning closer, her lips claimed his mouth.

And he was lost. In an instant. One touch of those sensuous lips and he had no way of stopping from kissing her. Kissing and wrapping his arms around her, bringing her as close as it was humanly possible for two people to get while sitting in chairs. And it still wasn't close enough. Without letting her go, he stood up, taking Claire with him, bringing her even nearer to his body. Still not near enough. There were clothes in the way. They needed to be one, melded together.

Her grip tightened around him, as though she felt the same need. His heart sang, and his head spun. This was beyond anything he'd experienced, or could remember experiencing. No, it was new. Claire had snagged his heart when he wasn't looking, and there was no way he was getting it back in a hurry, if he even wanted to. Which, right now, he doubted would ever come about.

She lifted her mouth, whispered, 'Nicolas,' in such a husky voice his toes curled, and then went back to kissing all reason out of him.

'Mummy... Where are you?' A tiny voice crept through the mist in his head.

He pulled away at the same moment as Claire jerked back. Looking around, he found Mia sitting up on the couch, staring around the room, her sleep-filled eyes wide open.

'I'm here, sweetheart.' With a wry smile, Claire headed into the lounge. 'What's up?'

'I want to go home.'

'We will shortly. Mummy and Nicolas are finishing their drinks and then I'll help clean up. Curl up and try to get some more sleep, sweetheart.'

'I want to go now.'

'Mia, lie down and close your eyes. I won't be long. Nicolas has been good to you and we don't just walk out without helping him.'

There was a don't-argue-with-me element to that voice Nicolas hadn't heard before. It made him smile. Claire wasn't too soft with her girl all the time.

'You can go. There's not a lot to be done in the way of cleaning up the kitchen.' But his body was calling out for another kiss. That wasn't happening tonight. 'As you said earlier, Mia's very tired.'

'We'll be home before eight and since it'll be Sunday she can sleep in tomorrow. She's not used to being out like this.'

Claire not having been dating or in a relationship recently saddened him, but it also made him happier to know she wasn't hankering after another man, and that she was free to date.

'We'll have to give her plenty of practice.' Was he rushing them both? Probably, but he couldn't help it. No doubt about it, his caution was easing. Claire was special, and the idea of walking away from her turned him cold.

'If you're willing,' he added, to show he was open to hearing how she felt.

Coming close, she brushed a quick kiss over his swollen lips. 'More than willing.'

And so ended a wonderful day, Nicolas sighed as he waved them off and closed the door. There'd be more to come. He just knew it. He might find an excuse to call around to Claire's tomorrow, just for the chance of seeing her.

Did he need an excuse? What was wrong with turning up and saying hi? It was what people did with family and friends, so why not turn up unannounced to see the woman who was changing his perspective on his future?

Done. Or it would be tomorrow. He would visit Claire. Spend some time together. Roll on tomorrow.

'How was your weekend, Claire?' Joachim asked on Monday morning.

'Fabulous. We went to the beach on Saturday, followed by a barbecue, and on Sunday we went to a vineyard for lunch. The sun shone all weekend and nothing could've been better.'

There was such a happy note in her voice that Nicolas found himself smiling as he perused the patient list in the triage office while the docs were yarning in the doorway to one of their rooms. Sounded to him like Claire had enjoyed their time together as much as he had.

'We? You have a partner?' Joachim asked. 'I thought you were single and that's why Nicolas drove you to the work party.'

'We as in me and Mia, and Nicolas.' She still sounded happy, so she wasn't feeling under pressure about having been with someone she worked with.

'I'm not surprised. You and Nicolas were inseparable that night,' Joachim said.

Nicolas's smile widened as warmth snuck under his ribs. Claire wasn't afraid to put their friendship out there. They weren't quite at the partnership stage, and if pushed he wouldn't have called her his partner either. They were getting there. But he cared for Claire so much he couldn't imagine not seeing a lot of her outside work, or never kissing her again, or not sharing a meal on his deck.

They weren't rushing round madly like young people in love. There was seriousness to their burgeoning relationship, an understanding that they had things to consider about each other and their own pasts. There was also a lot of laughter and fun, and sharing anecdotes about their careers and lives outside work, and occasionally about their pasts without touching the bad stuff.

Claire was still talking to Joachim. 'Moving to Blenheim is turning out to be marvellous. I'm loving the area and the people I'm getting to know.'

Loving the people. That was better. Nicolas bit his bottom lip to stop the grin that was trying to take over his face. Clicking onto the list of patients, he opened the first one.

Jody White, thirty-two, itchy rash on back and abdomen.

He stepped into the waiting area. 'Jody?'

A tired-looking woman with a puffy red face stood up. 'That's me.'

'Come through. I'm Nicolas, the triage nurse.' As he closed the door and pointed to the chair by the desk, he asked, 'Do you have a history of skin rashes or reactions to certain foods?'

'No, never.'

The day was underway. Nicolas found himself humming as he filled in patient details or when he was walking back from taking someone through to Radiology. He loved this job, but today it felt even better. There was a new spring in his step as he went about the clinic. When he wasn't behind a closed door assessing a patient he often heard Claire talking or laughing.

Everything kept coming back to Claire. She

made him feel alive, and filled with hope. He hadn't been down or unhappy before he'd met her, but these days he felt like a new man.

'Nicolas, can you give me a hand with Archie?' Claire stood in the doorway, looking worried.

The little boy he'd prioritised minutes ago because of a high heart rate and flushed face.

'I don't like his heart rate and need help monitoring him. According to his father he has shortness of breath when he's moving around and isn't interested in eating very much.'

They were in a quiet spell with no one waiting to be triaged.

'Archie had a respiratory virus a couple of weeks ago.' Viruses could lead to myocarditis.

'I saw that. Can you set up the monitor while I listen to his lungs again?'

'Hey, Archie. Let's get you onto the bed, eh?'

The two-year-old pushed in against his father, his eyes lacklustre.

'Come on, Archie. Nicolas is going to help you find out why you didn't eat your favourite breakfast.' Dad laid his son on the bed and held his hand while Nicolas lifted his shirt and placed the monitor tabs on the tiny chest.

Claire stepped up. 'Archie, I'm going to listen to your heart.' She rubbed the end piece. 'I hope this won't be too cold on your skin.'

Archie's skin was hot as he gasped for air, not filling his lungs enough with such short breaths.

'Dad?'

'It's okay, Archie. Everyone's here to make you better.'

'How ill was Archie with the RSV?' Claire asked after she'd listened to the boy's chest.

'Tired, listless and grouchy, otherwise not too bad,' the father answered. 'He's been worse these past couple of days.'

Sitting at her desk, Claire added some notes to Archie's file. Then she faced the father. 'Len, I believe your son has myocarditis, which is an inflammation of the heart muscles, and likely a follow-on from the virus.'

Len went white. 'How serious is this? It's his heart, I mean, what the...?'

'Sit down and I'll explain. People with mild myocarditis are more often than not treated at home. But because of Archie's age and his general lethargy I am going to have him admitted to the hospital to be on the safe side.'

Len was taking deep breaths. 'Could I have done something earlier? Was there something I should've noticed?'

Claire shook her head firmly. 'I don't think

so. Initially his symptoms would've been similar to recovering from the virus. It's only when the inflammation got worse would his breathing and listlessness have become more apparent. You said you brought him in here this morning because you noticed that when he woke up.'

'True, but what if I'd taken him to the emergency department last night? Would that have been better for him?'

'I can't answer that, except to say you hadn't noticed anything going on, and therefore had no reason to bring him out at night.' She paused, then smiled. 'Being a parent's hard, isn't it? Remember, you're not a doctor or nurse. You did your best, and Archie's no worse off for spending last night in his own bed.'

Nicolas felt his own heart tightening at her words. Claire was so good at this. She calmed patients, and treated people with respect. Turning back to Archie, he read the monitor. No changes to the heart rate. He hadn't expected any, but there was no such thing as too vigilant.

'Thanks, Doctor. You're not making me feel any better, but I'm grateful for your kindness, and your honesty.' Len returned to watching over his son.

Claire picked up the phone. 'Hi, Nola. It's

Claire McAlpine from the Urgent Care medical centre. I'm sending you a two-year-old with myocarditis.'

Nicolas tuned out and focused on his patient. 'I'm going to take you for a ride on the bed, Archie. Dad's coming with us too.' But first he needed to let the other nurses know he would be away for a short while. Someone else could cover triage. This boy wasn't going anywhere without him. 'Be right back. You hang in there.'

Claire handed him a sheet of paper the moment he returned. 'Here's the admittance form. We're in luck. The paediatric heart specialist is visiting from Nelson right now.'

His mouth curved into a smile. 'The more on our side the better.' Not that Archie probably needed to see a specialist, but the kid was only two and didn't need to have any further heart problems to deal with in the coming years.

'You're onto it.' She smiled in return.

Did his smile make her stomach tighten and her blood heat as hers did to him? He hoped so.

CHAPTER SEVEN

TWO DAYS BEFORE Christmas and it was date night. Claire sighed happily as she studied herself in the full-length mirror. Once again she and Nicolas were going out for dinner and Michelle was babysitting Mia. This time the teen was driving herself here, and wouldn't need a lift home afterwards.

It shouldn't make any difference to how she felt about going out with Nicolas, but damn, it did. It meant they could share time together back here afterwards, away from other people. Could share some of those devastating kisses, or more. More? Yes, well, how was she to know how she'd feel when they returned from the restaurant?

Since you already seem to know, what's with the question?

Claire laughed to herself. The black lacy G-string and low-cut bra were new. The olive-green dress with string straps and a deep vee partially revealing her breasts and flowing over her hips had been hanging in the window of Blenheim's most upmarket shop when she'd gone into town in her lunch break to pick up a book she'd ordered. The moment she'd seen the dress, she'd had to have it. Thank goodness it fitted perfectly or she'd have been disappointed beyond reason.

She'd been twenty minutes late getting back to work, but not even the annoyed look from Ryan had put a dent in her excitement. She worked extra time pretty much every day, and today had been the only time she'd ever taken longer for her break than she was meant to. Because it was date night. Nicolas did this to her. Making her toss caution to the breeze. Bring on more. She'd never felt like dancing so much. Her toes constantly tapping whenever she sat at her desk, hearing his voice as he talked to patients in his office.

Going out with Nicolas—again—got her adrenalin flowing and her head spinning. This was nothing like the flings she'd had. Nothing whatsoever. This was real, in that they were interested in getting to know each other. She grinned. Embracing how the other kissed, and how it felt to be held in one another's arms. Hopefully there'd be a lot more to experience very soon, because she didn't think she could hold out much longer. She didn't want to. She was ready to go further. Of course to have sex, but for her, with Nicolas, that meant a deeper, more personal knowledge of him.

Date night just got a whole lot more interesting and thrilling. Every time she thought about Nicolas her knees wobbled, her sex heated and her heart tripped.

'Mummy, Michelle's here.' Mia bounced into the bedroom looking as happy as her mother felt.

'Great. Tell her to come inside, will you?' The sound of another vehicle in the driveway had her heart revving. Nicolas had arrived. One last flick of her hair and she left the bedroom, ready for the evening, whatever it entailed. As long as it was fun, warned a little voice in the back of her head, causing her to trip. Why wouldn't they have fun? What could possibly go wrong? They got on so well.

'Hi, Claire.' Michelle stood inside the door.

'Come through, Michelle. Thanks for doing this. I really appreciate it.'

'Any time. Mia's fun, and I like looking after her.' The teen followed her bouncing charge into the lounge.

Turning back to the front door, her lungs stalled at the sight of him standing on her doorstep. Dressed in a cream open-necked shirt and tan trousers, his hair brushed away from his face, Nicolas looked breath-taking.

'Hi,' she managed in a quiet voice.

'Hello to you too. You look stunning,' he added, his face serious.

Money well spent, she decided. 'Th-thanks. Come in. Do you want a drink before we leave?'

'I don't think so. We're due at the restaurant in half an hour. I'll say hello to Mia and Michelle, then we should get on our way. It's a little way out of town, on the other side.'

'Nicolas!' Mia came racing out of the lounge, stopping directly in front of him.

'Hello, you. How was preschool?'

'Good. I drew a picture of what my new kitchen will look like. I'm going to leave it in the letterbox for Santa.'

First Claire had heard. Her girl was persistent, she'd give her that.

'I'm sure he'll find it, sweetheart.' As long as there wasn't a picture of a father giving her a hug.

Nicolas looked over to her, understanding in his eyes.

So he'd had the same thought, had he? They were in sync so often it was a little scary. What if he could read her mind on other topics when he was near? Like sex. She winced. It was all right. Those thoughts had occurred while she was in her bedroom and Nicolas hadn't arrived.

Mia spun around. 'It's on the table. Come on.'

Nicolas brushed Claire's hand as he walked past. 'Have you seen this?' he asked with a gentle smile.

'No. A great lookalike, for sure.'

'The right colour?'

'Sort of.' Now she was laughing, which had probably been his intention in the first place.

'Here. See?' Mia held up the picture that looked something like a storm with pots and plates in the air.

'It looks good.' Nicolas scuffed Mia's head. 'I can see you're an artist in the making.'

'I'm good, aren't I?'

'Yes, you are. Now, do I have your permission to take Mummy out for dinner?'

'I think so.'

Claire could see Mia's eyes lighting up with hope that there might be something in this for her.

'You can have one chocolate Santa before you go to bed in half an hour's time, missy. That's all.' Scooping her up into her arms, she kissed her girl on both cheeks. 'Be good for Michelle. I'll check up on you when I get home.'

'Have fun, Mummy.'

'I'm going to.'

'You seem certain about having fun,' Nicolas said as they settled at the table in the restaurant.

'Why wouldn't I be?' she replied, laughing. 'Unless you've got a hidden agenda of turning this into a night of torture and torment, I fully intend having a wonderful time.'

'You're safe.' He reached for her hand. 'Let's start with a glass of wine.'

'Perfect.' The restaurant was crowded, and the waiters were rushing around trying to keep up. More time to spend with this man. 'What have you been doing today?' It had been one of his days working in the vineyard, and she'd missed him at work. Something she'd keep to herself.

'Helped Bodie with some bud pruning. His grapes are coming on well. This is the quietest time of the year, more a watching phase and hoping the weather doesn't go wrong and we get too much rain.'

'When does harvest start?'

'Around the beginning of March, though there are some varietals that get hand-picked before then. Neither Bodie nor I have those.'

'So you'll be crazy busy come autumn?'

'You have no idea. Little sleep, lots of checking crops and decision-making on when to pick. Crazy is the right way to describe it. While my vineyard is small, I also work with Bodie on his.'

'So you don't work at the medical centre at all during harvest.' Hard to imagine the place without him. Even now, the two days a week he worked on the vineyard seemed to drag out. How would she survive a month or more?

'It's part of my contract to take weeks off at that time of the year. Management find someone to take my place so I don't have to feel bad about not being there.'

'Evelyn says she works fewer hours too because Bodie doesn't have time to look after Kent when he's not at preschool.'

'I think you'll find a lot of the businesses in town juggle their staff during harvest. It's the way of it, and no one really complains as the industry brings so much wealth to the area.' Nicolas looked over at the waiter approaching their table. 'Chardonnay? Or something else?'

'Chardonnay, thanks.' They were dining at another vineyard, and she wanted to try their wine. Picking up the menu, she perused the options, and sighed. 'How am I supposed to choose one dish when there are at least three I'd like to try?'

After their orders had been taken, she relaxed back in her seat and looked at Nicolas. He really was gorgeous.

'Did you ever see yourself being a wine grower when you were training to be a nurse?'

'Not once. Though I admit to a restlessness that I didn't understand for a while. Then I realised as much as I enjoyed nursing I also enjoyed being outside doing physical work. I missed that from the fishing years. When Bodie said there was land up for grabs next to him, it was a no-brainer.'

'Now you have the best of both worlds. How many people can say that?'

'Not many, I guess. What about you? Why medicine? Was it something you always wanted to do?'

'Nope. I was going to be a vet. Nothing or nobody was going to change my mind. I adored animals, and in the school holidays I worked at the local animal care centre, looking after cats and dogs mostly.'

Didn't most teenage girls with an aptitude for science want to be a vet? She'd been one of four in her class at high school who had. Only one had gone on to follow her dream.

'What changed your mind?'

'Watching a vet put down the most beautiful dog I adored and was pestering my mother to let me adopt. It was attacked by another dog, which had managed to escape from its cage when one of the helpers didn't fasten the latch properly. The injuries were terrible. Both dogs were put down that day. I cried for hours, and the end result was I decided to be a doctor instead.'

His eyes widened and there was a bemused smile on those sexy lips.

She added, 'It's far worse losing patients, but somehow I've learned to cope. As do all medical staff or we wouldn't last very long in the job.'

His grin faded. 'You're right. It's the downside to our work.'

Thankfully the wine arrived just then, and they picked up their glasses at the same time.

Nicolas tapped his against hers. 'Here's to more dates, and less gloomy talk.'

'I agree.' To both. Sipping the Chardonnay, she sighed with delight. 'That's so good.'

'Isn't it? I haven't given you a sample of my Chardonnay yet.'

'Have you still got some over from last year?'

'There's a couple of bottles in my cellar to take to Christmas lunch. Be warned, Bodie will want you trying his wines too. You might be inundated with different wines on the day.'

'Not likely. I don't tend to get carried away

with drinking.' Not with Mia to keep an eye on. Nor was having a hangover the next day her idea of fun. 'But I look forward to trying yours.'

'You'd better.' His laughter tickled her insides. As did a lot of things about him.

Until he asked, 'Have you ever been in a serious relationship? A long-term one?'

Her instant reaction was to say no and close down, but she was starting to think he was already a part of her life that she wasn't willing to let go. She cared about him, more than a lot. So much she could feel love on the horizon. Time to open up a little. Deep breath and, 'One. We lasted three years before he left. I tend to have trust issues after that and how my dad left me.'

He leaned back, his steady gaze not wavering, instead fixing on her more directly. 'Understandable. Can you see yourself moving past those issues?'

With Nicolas, yes, she could. But. There was always a but. What if he let her down? Walked away once she'd handed her heart over? Left without a glance over his shoulder, never to be heard from again? And broke Mia's heart as well? Talk to him. How was he going to understand if she didn't?

'I'd like to think so.' Her breast rose as her lungs filled.

His gaze softened and he slid her glass towards her. 'You worry about Mia. It's only natural.'

The wine was cool on her tongue and reminded her not everything was bad. Especially Nicolas.

'No, I couldn't face the idea of heartbreak again so I stuck to having the occasional fling, Mia being the result of one. The man who fathered her all but ran when he learned I was pregnant. I wasn't asking for anything more than he recognise his child and take part in her life in some way.'

Plates of food appeared in her line of vision. She wasn't sure she was ready to eat. Talking about those things always got her stomach roiling.

Nicolas picked up her free hand and kissed her palm. 'Thank you for telling me. It helps to understand how you must feel about relationships and putting Mia first.'

Hadn't she said he was good at reading her?

'Thanks,' she squeaked. 'I am wary about love. But I so want to have it all,' she added with an attempt at a smile. She had a feeling it didn't come off very well when Nicolas tightened his hand around hers.

'You can,' he said quietly, then sat back. Taking his hand with him. 'Let's enjoy our meals before they get cold. This is what we came out for. And making the most of each other's company.'

'True.' So why ask about her relationship history? Was he starting to think they might get together permanently? Wasn't it too soon for that? *Tell that to your heart, Claire. You mightn't be admitting to love, but what other word describes the emotions that fill you day in, day out?*

'Eat,' Nicolas said, before taking a mouthful of his steak.

The salmon was delicious, as was the company. They laughed and talked all the way through the meal, no more deep questions asked or answered. Nicolas appeared relaxed, and not scared off by her lack of commitment in the past. Of course he saw her commitment to Mia, so possibly that helped. Claire got on with enjoying herself, putting her concerns aside. She could fall in love and have a great future. Yes, she could. And would, if she carried on like this.

'You coming in?' Claire asked Nicolas when he pulled up outside the house.

'Yes.' But he didn't open his door, instead

reached for her and drew her close. 'After this.' He proceeded to kiss her senseless. So easily.

She gave up all trace of resistance, let the wonder of those lips on her mouth, his tongue teasing hers, take over. She knew nothing other than Nicolas, his hands spread across her back, his chest pressed against her breasts, his out-doorsy scent, his strength and gentleness. His kiss went on for ever, deepening with every passing moment. Taking her on a ride of long-ing and love and wonder.

When he eventually pulled back and looked into her eyes, she knew. It was time to let go the past and move forward. To see where their relationship led. To make the most of every opportunity that presented itself with Nicolas. To take a risk. She took his hands in hers, and brushed a soft kiss over his lips.

'Come on. Inside and alone.' Apart from a hopefully sleeping Mia. Michelle would hit the road as soon as she went indoors. Then it would be her and Nicolas, free to follow up on those kisses. She reached behind for the door handle.

'Claire?' Nicolas ran a finger over her cheek. 'Are you sure? I do not want to rush you.' His body was tense, and if the front of his trou-sers was anything to go by he had a hard-on that needed dealing with. Yet he was offering to back off. What a man.

'I couldn't be more certain if I tried. Are you all right with that?'

'Ye-es.' He was out of the four-wheel drive and around to her door so fast her head spun keeping up.

Inside she became practical and talked to Michelle. 'Any problems with Mia?'

She got an eye-roll and a short reply. 'Are you kidding? She's never any trouble.'

'Just trying not to be the mother who thinks her child would never do anything wrong,' Claire said with a laugh as she paid Michelle. 'Thanks for looking after her.'

'Any time. See you on Christmas Day. Hey, Nicolas, catch you then too.'

'Right, kiddo.' He closed the door behind her and turned to Claire. 'You go check on Mia. I'll be waiting.'

Naturally that was the first thing she'd do. Nothing would be wrong with Mia, but she still had to see for herself, and give her a kiss and touch her baby.

'Back in a minute.'

'Don't rush.'

She looked him over and laughed. 'Really?'

Disappearing down to Mia's bedroom before he could come back with a wisecrack, she hugged herself. All was good in her world.

Very good, she corrected later. Nicolas had taken her in his arms and danced them down to her bedroom, kissing her all the way. Her throat, her shoulders, her arms. Sending the tingles heating her skin into overdrive.

Closing the door behind them, she began to unbutton his shirt, every button earning a kiss on his chest, his nipples, that flat, tight stomach. The gasps of passion as her tongue slid over his skin heightened her own awareness deep inside, filling her with desire and love. Tipping her over the edge into bliss. Holding him around the waist, she stepped backwards towards the bed, impatient to be naked and wound around him. Needing to know him completely.

'Claire.' Nicolas breathed her name as though it were gold. Looking at her with hunger, before his gaze drifted down to her cleavage and he leaned in to kiss and wind her even tighter. 'You are special.'

He made her feel special. Reaching behind, she fiddled with the zip on her dress.

'Let me.' His fingers brushed her hot skin, teasing, tantalising as he lowered the zip at an unbearably slow pace.

'Nicolas,' she whispered against his mouth. 'Come on. I can't bear this.'

'Oh, yes, you can.' His eyes lit up and his mouth curved into a heart-melting smile. 'We've got all the time it takes.'

She didn't need many seconds, let alone minutes. She was throbbing with need. So was Nicolas. When she undid the front of his trousers he was hard.

When he slid her dress off her shoulders and down her frame to her waist she briefly removed her hand from that heat to slip her arms free, then returned to holding him, rubbing up and down, and getting nearer to exploding with each caress.

Sinking onto the edge of the bed, she negotiated his trousers down those firm thighs to his knees and beyond. Then, leaning in to take him in her mouth, she felt his hands on her head, lifting her away.

'No, no, no. We'll do this together. I'm not coming before you, sweetheart.' Nicolas slid down onto the bed, wrapping her in his arms as he went and sprawling over the covers with her lying on top of him. His hands were between them, teasing her nipples until they were so hard she thought they'd explode.

'Don't stop,' she cried as she eased upward

and crouched over his throbbing manhood, touching the tip, feeling the zing of heat that brought on in her core. Again and again, until she had to let go, to cramp around him, and bring him to his peak. Sliding down his length, she filled herself with his need, and lifted up, lowered again.

'Claire,' he cried. 'Claire.'

And then she came, exploding around him, falling into his arms, against his bucking body. Into a world she hadn't known before. A wonderful, exciting, loving place. Somewhere she would want to come back to again and again. She'd found what she hadn't believed possible. They'd made love, not had sex. She'd let go all restraints and been given so much in return.

Curling up around Nicolas, she sighed with pure happiness. Anything was possible when she felt so good, so comfortable with Nicolas.

He moved, stretching his legs and lifting his arm from around her.

She held her breath. He wasn't leaving already? He couldn't. Unless—unless this had only been a quick release for him and he wanted no more. Her heart started to flutter. Not this time. Not Nicolas. Not that.

Nicolas leaned up on one elbow and traced a finger down her cheek, over her chin, across her neck and down between her aching breasts that hadn't known such erotic tension in forever.

'Claire, I don't know what to say. That was amazing. You are amazing.'

Her lungs expelled a breath and her heart rate returned to a semblance of normal. 'No more than you.' She smiled through her relief. 'I can't believe what just happened. I've never known anything quite like what we shared.' Honesty paid dividends, didn't it? If he understood how much their lovemaking meant to her then he wouldn't let her down. Would he?

'Relax, sweetheart. I'm not walking away from this. From you. This is a beginning, not the end.'

See? He read her so well it was scary at times. But not now. She'd needed to hear that. There were no words to describe her feelings, unless she was prepared to sound gushy and stupid. Taking his face between her hands, she brought their mouths together and kissed him with an intensity that said it all for her.

What else could she do? He'd turned her life upside down within weeks, and now she was ready to take a chance on him, on them. She wanted more, a lot more, and she had plenty to give back. It was a freeing moment. She, Claire McAlpine, wanted to share her life with this wonderful man. So much so that she was prepared to put her heart out there and see where it led.

Lying down beside her again, Nicolas reached for her and drew her in close. 'Thank you,' he said so quietly she strained to hear his words.

'For what?'

'Trusting me. Giving yourself to me, accepting me without question.'

So she wasn't the only one with doubts. There'd been plenty of questions, but in the end, 'It was easy.'

His hug tightened, and he rested his head against hers. 'Very.'

CHAPTER EIGHT

'FINALLY…' CLAIRE SIGHED.

Mia was hyped to the max. Santa was coming.

'She's really asleep? At last?' Nicolas asked with hope widening his eyes.

Sinking onto the couch beside him, she dared to smile. 'Yes. But I'll check shortly to be absolutely certain. She's shattered.'

'She might sleep in a little later than expected.' The hope was increasing.

'Christmas Day and a stocking waiting at the end of her bed filled with surprises? Get over yourself.'

'Not forgetting the present she's waiting for. She hasn't forgotten for a moment that Santa's bringing it, has she?'

'Nope.' But so far it seemed she had forgotten the hug she'd asked for.

'Let's hope she's completely absorbed with

it.' Nicolas dropped his arm over her shoulders and drew her nearer.

Claire mentally crossed her fingers. 'I have no idea what brought on that other request of Santa. She's never said anything like it before. She rarely mentions having a father and where hers might be.' Being more relaxed than ever with Nicolas had her opening up further about the things that bothered her. It was a new experience, and made her more comfortable with him and about herself and what she was looking for.

His hand was rubbing little circles on her shoulder. 'The questions will no doubt become more frequent as she gets older and understands most other kids have a father in their lives.'

'As long as she doesn't blame herself for Hank not being there for her.' The pain Mia would know would be very similar to what she'd experienced. Unless her mother fell in love and settled down with a man who adored her. Anyone come to mind?

She turned to Nicolas as he said, 'You still have a little time to think about how you're going to answer questions, and be as prepared as it's possible to get. She'll throw you some curve balls though.'

'No doubt at all.' Smiling at this man who was winning her heart all too easily with his understanding and care, she said, 'I can see you being a great hands-on dad. No walking away from the hard yards for you.'

'I'd like to think I'd do a good job.'

He most certainly would.

'How about some wine?' Before we go to bed. 'I hope you didn't make up the other spare bed for me.' Once upon a time she'd never have said that, but Nicolas made her so comfortable she found she often spoke from the heart and not the head.

'I didn't want to be presumptuous,' he said, laughing. 'But no, I took a chance and left it as it was.' He stood up. 'I'll get the wine. You stay there. You're looking exhausted.'

'It was busy at work today. Silly me thought it would be quieter with people out doing last-minute shopping for tomorrow.'

'Think about it. A lot of the patients we saw were older, and alone, as though they weren't going to be busy with family or friends to-morrow.' The glasses clinked as he took a pair from the cabinet.

'I hadn't thought of that.' They'd admitted two serious cases to hospital though. Patients with family at their sides the whole time they were in the medical centre. 'I can't believe I've got four days off.' As one of the newest doctors working there, she'd been lucky when Ryan had said he was happy to work if she wanted to take a break. It'd only taken seconds to accept. Spending more time with Mia—and hopefully Nicolas when he was available—was right up there with the best way to spend her day.

'Lucky you. I'm on the roster for the twenty-seventh and eighth.'

She'd seen that. 'I can be on cooking duty then.'

'Here, try this.' He passed her a glass of Sauvignon Blanc. 'It's one of Bodie's, and I hate to say it, but it's damned good.'

'Exceptional.'

'Damn it, knew you'd say that.' He returned to sit beside her and rested his free hand on her thigh. 'This is cosy.'

'Very.' Having quiet time with Nicolas and looking forward to Christmas Day with him and friends lightened her heart in a way she hadn't known for a long time, if ever. 'Where were you this time last year?'

'Sitting here, a wine in hand, and watching some nonsense on TV.'

That was a clear memory. Similar to hers, apart from the wine. It would've been tea.

'You don't join your family at this time of year?'

'Dad's gone and Mum's in a rest home. My brother and his lot go to his wife's family and take Mum with them. There're plenty of them and they're into massive gatherings, which make me feel the odd one out. Probably my own doing, but I prefer to stay away. I fly up to see Mum every couple of months. It's hard as she's got dementia.'

How sad. The few times he'd mentioned his family he hadn't sounded close to any of them.

'Actually, if I remember correctly, I was a bit melancholy last year, and the TV wasn't distracting me from thinking about my life and being single and what might lie ahead.' He sipped his wine as he stared at the floor beyond his feet. 'Just saying, you know.'

Leaning her head on his shoulder, she said, 'Yes, I know. Even knowing feeling sorry for yourself is a waste of time, it's not always possible to ignore the sense of being alone and thinking about others who are with family or friends.'

'Yet I've got the best mates down the road and I can go join them whenever I want. But sometimes I like to stay away and be strong and even enjoy that solitary time.' And give them space.

'It's what makes you strong. Stronger,' she amended before tapping his glass with hers.

'Here's to a merry Christmas and a very happy New Year.' One week to go and then another year would be starting. This time, for the first time, a sense of anticipation filled her. There was lots to look forward to. Her hand tightened over Nicolas's. Lots. Hopefully.

'Back at you, Claire.' His smile went straight to her heart, warming her throughout like nothing else could. 'Drink up and let's go to bed.'

The warmth turned to full-on heat. Right between her legs, in her fingers, over her skin. Definitely a Christmas like no other.

If this was how the last week of the year was panning out, bring on the New Year. It had to be even better.

Nicolas rolled over and sat up in his bed. Excited giggles were coming from the room next door.

Beside him, Claire blinked open her eyes. 'What's the time?'

Checking his phone, he groaned. 'Five ten.'

'Great,' she groaned. 'I'd better get up before Mia comes looking for me.'

'Yes, we kind of messed up there.' They'd agreed last night that it was too soon for Mia to find them in bed together, even if she didn't understand what it really meant. Come to think of it, he wasn't one hundred percent certain what it meant either. He and Claire had become lovers very quickly, and deep down he knew there was a lot more to this than just getting together for sex. He didn't know how much more, and what he wanted. Apart from love and a long-term future. But was Claire the other half of that picture? He hoped so. Yet something was pulling at him, telling him to be careful. *Go slow, be certain, don't get hurt.*

'I'll go put the kettle on for a brew.'

'I'll go see what Santa's delivered.' Her grin was tired but still knocked him sideways.

'Go, Mum.' They'd moved the kitchen set into the lounge by the Christmas tree last night, but there were a couple of small parcels on the end of Mia's bed.

Slipping her satin robe over that sensational body, Claire shook her head. 'Any minute Mia'll be saying Santa's let her down. There isn't a kitchen.' Placing a kiss on his cheek, she smiled. 'Santa delivered a lot that I enjoyed during the night.'

Returning the kiss, he pulled on shorts and tee-shirt. 'He had a delightful helper.'

'Corny,' she groaned through her smile.

'Mummy!' Mia shrieked down the hallway. 'Santa forgot my kitchen.'

'Told you.' Claire laughed. 'Mia, it might've

been too big to put in the bedroom. Have a look by the Christmas tree.'

Nicolas stepped out of the door. 'Merry Christmas, Mia. Santa won't have forgotten.'

'Coming, Mummy?'

'I wouldn't miss this for anything.' Claire grinned and snatched up her phone.

With Mia racing down the hall, he took Claire's hand and followed. Warmth and gentleness emanating from Claire caused his heart to melt. Mia's excitement got to him too. This was what having a family must feel like. Breathtaking wonder. If the rest of the day turned out to be boring, it didn't matter. This was the best it could be.

Wrong, it got better when Mia spied her present. All hell broke loose in the form of one small girl charging at the tree and the presents stacked around it. 'My kitchen's here! Mummy, look what Santa brought me.'

Tears were streaking down Claire's cheeks as she bit her bottom lip.

Nicolas had to blink back some of his own. This woman was such a loving mother. As well as a great big softie. He wound his arms around her and kissed the top of her head. 'You're special.'

Mia tore the wrapping paper off and giggled. 'Did you see that, Nicolas? Santa's cool.'

'Claire, give me your phone or there won't be any photos.'

She blinked, and handed it over. 'Take plenty. Then I'm going to make some tea.'

'Good idea. We're due over the fence at nine. On past experience, breakfast will be large, but right now a mug of tea sounds ideal.' Claire didn't sit around expecting to be waited on. She got stuck in with anything that needed to be done. Then again, she was used to living without a partner so no magical house fairy doing the chores.

'Does Evelyn go all-out for Christmas?'

'Breakfast, followed by presents and coffee, then mid-afternoon lunch. Usually one or two neighbours who have nowhere else to go drop in. Strays and waifs, Evelyn calls them.'

'Do Mia and I fit into that category?' she asked with a small smile.

'Hardly. You're her friend. And mine.' Friend? Yes, and now lover. 'A very special friend.'

'A friend with benefits?' Her smile was turning cheeky.

'Better.' And that, Nicolas told himself, was enough. He still didn't know where they were going with their relationship, only that he was loving every moment he spent with Claire. 'I take my tea black.'

'I think I've seen you make it often enough at work to know that.'

So she observed the most ordinary things about him. What else had she noted? Anything important? Like how he didn't care about trying to impress her around his house? He hadn't spent hours dusting and vacuuming yesterday. Not that there'd been time, but he did know of people who'd stay up half the night preparing for visitors. What a waste of sleep time.

'Do you want something to eat, Mia? Breakfast's a long time away.'

'Santa put some chocolate in my stocking. I'm going to eat that.'

Nicolas glanced at her mother, and had to laugh at the resignation on her face.

'Walked into that one, didn't I?' Claire said. 'Mia, don't eat all of it. Keep some to share with Kent.'

'Fat chance.' Nicolas went across to the small decorated tree he'd put up before going to work yesterday so that Mia didn't miss out. 'Let's see what's under here, shall we?'

'Are there more presents for me?' Mia bounced beside him, her kitchen momentarily forgotten.

'There might be.'

After she'd gone to sleep last night Claire had put a few parcels under the tree. From her friends for Mia, she'd said. He'd felt a little sad that there were none from family, because there wasn't a family other than her mum. And a grandmother in Perth, who didn't seem to have sent a parcel.

I want a cuddle from my daddy.

Those words rang loud in his head. Would he never forget them? Mia was such a happy kid, always laughing and talking, making her request even more shocking now he knew her a little.

'Let me see. What does this one say? Um…' He scratched his chin. '"To Mia, love from Mummy".' He held out the present, to have it snatched from his hand.

'Mia, don't snatch, and say thank you to Nicolas.' Stern mother on the job.

'Thanks, Nicolas.' The wrapping paper was flying in pieces, no delicate unwrapping going on.

'Wow, Mummy, this is cool.' Mia held up a pink bikini and pink beach towel. 'I love it.' Leaping at Claire, she wound her arms tight around her neck and plonked a kiss on her cheek. 'Thanks, Mummy.'

Nicolas picked up a small package. 'Merry Christmas, Claire.'

Locking beautiful toffee-brown eyes on him, she said, 'This really is Christmas, isn't it?' Her smile was tentative, as though she worried she'd said too much.

'It is indeed.' Glancing to see if Mia was distracted by her bikini, he leaned down to brush a light kiss on Claire's cheek. 'It's wonderful to be sharing the day with you both.'

'I can't imagine anything better.' Her fingers worked at the tape on the small package, first one piece then the next, then the wrapping paper was unfolded from around the small box. She looked from the jewellery box to him and back. Her breasts lifted as she drew a breath and opened the box to expose the delicate gold chain he'd chosen.

'Oh, Nicolas, it's beautiful.' Her fingers shook as she picked up the chain and laid it on her palm. 'Beautiful.' There was a hitch in her voice.

'I hope it's your sort of thing.' She'd worn a copper necklace when they'd gone out to dinner the first time, but he hadn't noted her wearing other jewellery, apart from that ring on her finger.

The look she gave him made his heart beat faster. 'It's absolutely my thing.' Holding the necklace out, the clasp undone, she said, 'Would you do the honours?'

'Try and stop me.' Her neck was warm against his clumsy fingers as he worked the tiny clasp. 'There.' The gold chain looked perfect against her lightly tanned skin. He wanted to swing her up in his arms and race down to the bedroom. Instead he drew a steadying breath and stepped back. The one drawback to having her daughter with them, one that didn't really bother him, apart from the tightness in his groin that wasn't going to be satisfied any time soon. He gave her a lopsided grin instead, and got one in reply.

'Mummy, can I see?' Mia pushed between them, her little face close to Claire. 'It's pretty, Nicolas.'

'I'm spoilt, aren't I?' Claire whispered something in Mia's ear, who then raced to the tree. 'Thank you so much,' Claire said against his mouth before following up with a quick kiss.

'Nicolas, this is for you. From me and Mummy.'

Groaning inwardly at the interruption that was to be expected, he laughed and took the proffered present from Mia. 'What's this?'

'A surprise,' she told him.

It certainly was. A leather-bound copy of a book he'd been telling Claire about a couple of weeks back. He hadn't been able to track down a copy anywhere online or in the local second-hand stores.

'Where did you find this?' he asked in amazement.

Her forefinger tapped her nose. 'That's for me to know.'

'And me to find out,' he rejoined with a chuckle. Bending down, he touched Mia's shoulder lightly. 'Thank you very much for my present, little one.' Hugs were out of the question since the Santa debacle. He was too aware of upsetting Mia. But he could hug her mother. 'Thank you too. I can't believe you managed to track down a copy. I'll treasure this for ever.'

'You'd better.' She grinned. 'Now for that tea.'

The rest of the day continued in the same comfortable, happy way, with everyone having fun opening presents and eating too much salmon, ham and salads, along with pavlova and fresh fruit salads, and chocolate that seemed to disappear in a hurry, mainly gobbled up by two youngsters joined at the hip and their new toys to play with.

'It's been quite the day,' Nicolas said to Claire as they entered his house in the evening, trailed by an exhausted Mia.

'I don't remember a Christmas like it,' Claire admitted. 'Everyone was so relaxed. No arguments or grizzles. Definitely a first.'

He hated to think what that meant. Even in his family Christmas had always been a load of fun when he was a boy. They'd only got off-kilter when he and his brother became young adults with their own agendas, and his hadn't fitted the mould of perfect son.

'Here's to more like it.' If he had his way, they'd definitely be sharing more.

'Nicolas, I want a cuddle.' Mia stood right in front of him, leaning back, her big brown eyes staring up at him.

About to reach down to lift her up into his arms, Nicolas felt his heart thump hard. He paused, gazed down at Claire's daughter. Longing filled her eyes. Longing for something he wasn't sure he could deliver. A hug, yes, but what about what might be behind that hug? Would he be starting something that he wasn't ready for? None of them were ready for? If Mia saw it as more than a friendly gesture he could end up breaking her little heart. Something he had no intention of doing.

'Santa didn't bring me the one I asked for.'

Pain slammed his chest. His heart. Banging like crazy. He was not this kid's father. As much as he thought she was adorable, he was not taking on that role to make her happy. He wasn't even pretending to make up for the man missing in her life. Not until he and Claire knew where they were headed, and they had a way to go there, despite getting on so well together. He was falling for Claire but that didn't mean he was prepared to take a risk on his heart. Nor Claire's and Mia's.

'Come here, Mia. I've got a hug for you.' Claire held her arms out to her daughter, her face frozen with shock.

'I want one from Nicolas. He hugs you all the time. Why can't he hug me?'

Put like that, why was he hesitating? Because it felt wrong when this child longed for her father to pick her up and hold her. Because the look on Claire's face said she had a problem with what her girl wanted of him. Or was the shock because of Mia's request, not his delay in responding?

Mia stamped her foot. 'Don't you like me, Nicolas?'

He couldn't hold back any longer. 'Of course I do. Come here.' Sweeping her up, he held her close, and tried not to let the feel of her little arms winding around his bigger ones make him think he could step up to replace her father. He was not ready for that and, judging by Claire's face, neither was she. Mia certainly wasn't. What if he and her mother didn't last as a couple? Couple? They might be dating and spending quite a lot of time together, but were they even officially a couple yet? He had no idea. He wanted that, except now he doubted they would ever make the grade. Too much at stake. He'd known what the risks were but this was reality slamming into him, waking him up.

Claire reached for Mia, took her out of his arms and gave her a mummy hug, before saying, 'It's getting late and time we went home.' She didn't look at him as she put Mia down and headed down to his bedroom where her overnight bag was.

He followed. 'You don't have to go. You can stay the night.'

Tossing her few possessions into her bag, she said, 'I need some space. It's been a big day, Nicolas.'

Couldn't argue with that, but it had been a fantastic day. As had the night before. But… 'Nothing to do with the pain showing on your face?' Pain that said she didn't trust him enough to keep her and Mia safe. Or that she didn't love him and had realised she shouldn't be here?

Everything to do with what I'm feeling. She'd made a right mess of things.

'Nothing at all,' she lied. 'Mia did surprise me a little. Again. Which suggests to me she needs to be home catching up on sleep.'

Claire swallowed her panic. What now? Think everything through before she put her foot right in it. Keep quiet when she couldn't find a suitable answer, one that wouldn't tell Nicolas more than she was ready for. The day had followed on from such an intimate night she'd let go the brakes on her dreams and had a wonderful time with him. Hours of amazement, of fun, of sharing everything, of just being together. Hours when she'd forgotten to put Mia first.

All because she'd fallen in love with Nicolas when she hadn't been looking. Slam, bang, head over heels in love. It wasn't meant to happen, shouldn't have transpired, and yet her heart was full with love for him. She had to get away before any more damage was done. Before she said something she couldn't take back.

She wasn't ready, probably never would be. Nor was Mia. She wanted a father, but that wasn't Nicolas's role to fill. He wasn't ready for a full-on relationship with her, and therefore not with Mia either. He mightn't have meant anything by his hug than to make Mia happy, but her girl would see it as far more. Hope would start growing and she'd soon put more demands on him. It wasn't happening when there was no guarantee pain wouldn't follow.

Tugging at the zip on the bag, an ache formed in her chest. What had she done? Gone and hurt two people, all because she'd let her dreams get in the way of common sense. Because love had snuck in when she hadn't been looking.

Get me out of here.

'I'll put the doll's kitchen in your car.' Nicolas spoke softly, before striding away as though he suddenly couldn't wait to be shot of her.

Who could blame him? He was probably keen on a fling, and now the realisation of what that really meant was hitting home. Just as hard as the realisation she had fallen in love with Nicolas slammed her.

Talk about a double whammy. *I had no intention of loving him.* But she did. *Get out of here. Now. Fast. Go home and be safe.* Too late.

All she could hope was that it wasn't too late for Mia. Or was that being selfish? Was she using Mia as an excuse not to lay her heart on the line? To expose her vulnerability?

Damn, oh, damn. What now? How did she cope? She and Nicolas had to work together. Be calm around each other. Hardly going to act like a demented hen, was she? Possibly not. But how did she get through the days pretending to herself Nicolas meant nothing more than a nurse she'd had a few wonderful days with? Was there a self-help book to show her how to cope?

Claire buckled Mia into her car seat. 'Good night, Nicolas,' she said softly, meaning goodbye to more days and nights like those they'd just shared.

'Goodnight, Nicolas,' Mia shouted. 'I had fun today.'

He poked his head inside the car. 'Nightnight, little one. I had fun too.' Then he straightened and locked his eyes on Claire. 'I mean it.'

'I'm sorry,' she repeated quietly. 'This is me being strong for my daughter.' That was an excuse, and she sensed he knew it. At least he'd never guess what she was really feeling, how she'd gone and fallen in love with him. That would be too much. It would never work.

'Mia is one very lucky girl,' he replied just as quietly.

See? He wasn't as involved in this relationship as she was. He wasn't in love with her. They'd had a brief fling. Calling it quits had always been on the cards. Now it had happened. There was no returning to last night and the intimacy they'd shared, the warmth at being held in his arms as they lay naked in his bed. It was over—almost before it had started—but definitely over.

Claire headed around the car to her door, discreetly rubbing her cheeks with the back of her hand. 'I'll see you at work.' Should've taken that position in Auckland when it was on offer. But Blenheim had rung a lot of bells, and she couldn't in all honesty say she'd have preferred the large city. Her heart might still have been intact though.

Her hair swished across her face at her abrupt shake. Meeting Nicolas was the best thing to happen in a very long time. She couldn't deny it. Not even when the weeks and months ahead looked bleak.

Nicolas stood, hands on hips, watching Claire head down the long drive and out onto the road. All the time his body felt heavy and his head filled with longing. She had driven away with his heart in her hands, and no idea how much she meant to him.

Because you haven't had the guts to tell her. He'd only really understood minutes ago. Right when she'd said she needed space. As though she'd had enough of him. Wanted to seek solitude, and didn't need him sitting beside her, sharing a wine or holding hands.

I'll see you at work. Claire's words rang in his ears, reminding him how he had not wanted a relationship in the first place. He'd believed they might share a few days and nights together and then it'd be over, no regrets. The regrets were already swamping his heart. Not once had he believed he could fall in love again, and yet here he was, his heart heavy with love. He trusted Claire more than he'd thought he'd ever trust again.

Now she was gone. Out of his life. She hadn't said as much, but he knew her well enough to know she had no intention of returning to what they'd had going. It had been there in the protective way she'd held Mia. They were done. Except at the medical centre. That was going to be painful. Could they still work as a team after this? They had to. It might be the way to get back on track and start over. *I wish.*

She had warned him she didn't do relationships. He'd be naïve to think that didn't matter. He could hope she'd talk about this when she'd had time to think it through, but he knew Claire better than that. The barriers were up, locked in place. It would take more than a few words to bring them down again. No, best he worked at locking down his feelings and moving forward, denying his love and not putting his vulnerability out there. He knew all too well how that went. It was like being chopped off at the ankles with nothing to save him.

Claire had been quick to head away. Did

that mean she didn't trust *him*? It was possible, with her history. Did she think he wasn't good enough for her? Was he? What if he did get involved with Claire and then ended up leaving her? And her daughter? Yes, and what if they stayed together for the rest of their lives? How wonderful would that be? *I wish.*

He had a lot of wishes. Right now, after such a wonderful twenty-four hours, it was hard to believe none of them were coming true. The tail-lights on Claire's car as she disappeared around the corner rubbed it in. Gone for the night? Or out of his personal life for ever?

Was he really going to give up that easily? It wasn't in his nature to walk away from problems. He'd never avoided his father's insistence he do better at school. He'd merely reacted by showing how good he was at other things, which had so annoyed his parents they'd pressed down harder on him. When his ex had walked out on him, he'd shown her he wasn't hurting by getting on with his nursing training and buying the property he now lived on to forge a life on the land as well. He'd shown her he didn't need her to follow his dreams.

Did that mean Claire could drive away and he wouldn't do anything about the love he already felt for her?

No, it didn't.

This was something he wanted to fight for. Claire. Love. A life together. They'd only known each other for a short time but he knew she was the one for him. Might've known it the first time he'd seen her as she was aching for Mia, wanting to make it better for her daughter who was asking for a cuddle from her father.

The cuddle he'd been afraid to give tonight because he didn't want to hurt Mia, or Claire, or himself. His unconditional love for Mia had struck him hard. There'd been no compromise. When Claire had talked about the father and how he wanted nothing to do with his child even before she was born, the torment in her voice had cut through him like a knife through butter.

So, yes, he was going to fight for Claire.

But he'd go slowly, build up her trust, take it one long and slow day at a time. Somehow he'd manage to stay away from banging down her door and demanding they talk this through. Somehow he'd give her space and time to think about what they'd started. Hopefully she'd miss him as much as he was going to miss her. Working together would be hard—but do-able. It had to be.

What if it wasn't? Claire might not feel the

same about him. Then he'd be setting himself up for a big fall. But sitting back and doing nothing when his heart was so invested in her would be far worse.

Turning away from the view of the empty road, he headed inside, only to be met with the sight of the twinkling lights on the Christmas tree and screwed-up wrapping paper Mia had left behind a chair. He could hear her squeals of excitement and see Claire's laughter and relief as she tore the paper off the kitchen set. It had been fun putting that together last night, thinking about Mia's smile when she saw what Santa had brought. His heart beat faster as he remembered the morning, when he'd watched Claire open the box holding the gold chain he'd bought her, seeing her eyes light up and her delectable mouth curve into a soft, adorable smile directed at him.

I should never have let Nicolas get so close, Claire thought despondently as she tucked Mia into bed with her favourite doll. 'Goodnight, sweetheart.' She brushed stray strands of hair off Mia's face. Her girl was exhausted.

'Why didn't we stay with Nicolas?'

'We live here, sweetheart. We have to come home at the end of the day.' Did they though? She could've taken her time and not reacted instantly to protect her heart. Then who would? There was no one else for that job.

'We stayed there last night.'

'Because it was Christmas.'

Please don't throw a tantrum, kiddo. I'm about done for the day. No energy left in the tubes.

Admittedly, most of that had been used up enjoying herself with Nicolas and the others. It had been the best Christmas she'd ever experienced. She'd learned how special the day could be when spent with those who accepted her for who she was, and her heart had been fully focused on the people she'd shared it with, including Mia and Nicolas.

Funny how both names seemed almost linked in her heart now. Then it had all fallen to pieces. Because she'd let it. She'd panicked when Mia demanded that hug. She'd been afraid Nicolas would wake up to what he might be getting himself into. Because she'd suddenly realised how deeply in love with him she was, and that nothing was ever going to be the same. To give her heart away meant trusting him implicitly. Which she did. Or she thought she did. She was afraid to find out the true answer. Mia might be hurt. *She* would be.

'It's not fair,' Mia said through a big yawn.

Damn right it wasn't fair. Nicolas was *the* man. But he wasn't ready, and might never be.

'You can't always get what you want, little one.'

Nicolas had called Mia 'little one' earlier. As if he cared about her daughter. But that didn't mean he wanted the whole package. He had to love her for that and, despite how close they'd become, she couldn't say whether or not he felt that way about her. Or was she trying too hard to appease herself? Hard to deny her distrust of men though. Yet it hadn't taken long to fall in love with this particular one. He was everything she'd dreamed of, and more. Last night, lying in his bed against him, had been the best thing in a long time.

Bed. The idea of curling up under a sheet had seemed sublime an hour ago. Now she'd be alone, not tucked against Nicolas's hot, sexy body, caressing his skin, kissing his chest, making the most of being with the wonderful man who had opened her eyes to the possibility of a future where she wasn't raising Mia on her own but one where she gave her heart away and was loved deeply in return.

Filling the kettle, she stared out of the window onto the back yard. It was so small and ordinary after the wide green landscape that was Nicolas's vineyard. The kitchen was poky but practical, as was the rest of the house. Other homes surrounded the property on three sides. So close there wasn't a lot of privacy. At least it wasn't going to be her permanent abode. She'd rented so that she'd have time to get to know Blenheim better and decide where she'd like to live. Unfortunately so far she hadn't seen anything that compared with the rural location where Nicolas lived. Evelyn and Bodie's property was equally enchanting, which might suggest she'd like a house a little way out of town. Were there any houses out there that didn't come with acres of land requiring a lot of upkeep?

Get real, Claire.

She'd never lived anywhere but in a city, with neighbours all around, and a small lawn and few gardens to maintain. What would she know about the countryside? But there had to be some small properties, surely? It could be exciting living a little way out of town, with quieter roads and neighbours some distance away. What was she doing even thinking about this? A lot of her investments would be used in establishing her own practice later next year.

She poured boiling water over her tea bag. Stared as the water in the mug darkened. She was getting ahead of herself. It was a diversion from what had gone down between her and Nicolas at the end of a perfect day. Teach her for thinking her life had done a complete turnaround from how it usually ran. It went to show she was vulnerable when she wanted to find a new happiness involving a decent man, and a family life for her and Mia. When it started to look real, she'd done a runner.

I've only known Nicolas since the beginning of the month. What was I doing, thinking we might have a future?

How did she manage to fall in love so easily when she was so cautious? Not once did she stop and seriously think about what she was doing. It was too soon to be getting romantically involved. They didn't know each other well enough to be falling in love. Love was for ever, through the good and bad times, yet she'd wanted to go ahead. Nicolas had got to her in all sorts of ways, made her feel special and cared about, had her thinking about a better life and making her thankful for uprooting her life and moving here, but she wasn't ready to commit to for ever. She might want to, but it was so risky she was scared. It had been a brief interlude, exciting and sexy and had her waking up at night to pinch herself in case it was all a dream. Then her daughter had woken her up in a hurry by asking for a hug. No big deal really. It was normal. Except Claire knew it meant so much more, or could if she hung around too long. So she'd walked away before she could get badly hurt.

Too late, Claire. You're already hurting.

The idea that Nicolas mightn't care for her anywhere near as much as she did for him had her running for safety—aka these four walls. Brought on by memories of how the men in her past had all ignored her love, gone and left her to face life without them. Not that she'd loved Hank. Not at all, but he'd destroyed something huge for Mia, which was unforgivable.

She doubted Nicolas would ever do that, but he hadn't known them very long, and tonight had been a wake-up call for her. She couldn't risk waiting for him to fall for her because it might never happen. She had to protect their hearts. There was no one else who could do that.

Milk splashed on the bench as she poured.

Nicolas is the most amazing man I've known.

She didn't want to go days without seeing him, talking and sharing a joke, having a meal together.

She had to.

Great. They had to work together in the medical centre, discuss patients and treatment as though nothing was out of the ordinary. That was going to be hard—if not impossible. Every time she saw him she'd be remembering those arms around her, those lips on hers, his eyes filled with laughter as they talked.

Sitting on the tiny deck sipping her tea, her shoulders slumped as she sighed. This time next week would be New Year's Eve. A new year should bring wishes for the coming twelve months, wishes that included love and Nicolas. She'd dared to dream of a happy, fulfilled year. A year with him at her side, and the future opening up in front of them.

Now that seemed a stretch. A big one.

Her fingers ran along the chain around her neck. Nicolas had bought it for *her*. It was beautiful, special. It meant a lot. What was going on? Had the day been too good, and they'd both suddenly taken a step back, jolting each other mentally in the process?

It wasn't going to be easy not spending time with Nicolas. No making love, or kisses that were out of this world. In a very short time he'd given her so much she'd been missing for a long time. Had she ever known such enticing kisses or exciting sex? She must have. But she'd certainly forgotten all about them until Nicolas came along and stole into her heart.

But… She dragged oxygen into her lungs. Not one man she'd been close to had stuck with her in any way. The chances of Nicolas being

any different were slight, if her track record
was anything to go by.

Glancing at her finger, she saw her mother's ring. *I'm so proud of you.* Yes, she had to
continue being strong. She couldn't succumb
to her love for Nicolas. Not until she knew if
he was interested in going further, and then it
had to be the whole way. Mia wasn't getting
hurt because her mother wanted to love and be
loved by a wonderful man. Damn it, she didn't
want to get hurt either.

So they were over. Finished.

CHAPTER NINE

CLAIRE SANK DOWN in front of her desk to type in the last notes for the day. First day back after Christmas and it had crawled by. Much like the days she'd been off work. Not even taking Mia to the beach every day had made the hours speed up. She'd missed Nicolas even more than she'd have believed possible, as if a piece of her was gone for good.

Until this morning they hadn't spoken since Christmas night, which had been hard to take. Too often she'd picked up her phone to call him, then put it down again. She wanted to see him, share time with him, but she was also afraid of where it might lead, if she was truly ready to take that final step. Full-on commitment would be wonderful—if she could let go the past rejections and move forward without worrying about what might happen.

Here at work, Nicolas was his usual friendly self, though the sexy smiles and occasional touch on her shoulder had disappeared. At one point he'd brought her a mug of coffee when she hadn't had a chance to take a five-minute break. 'Get that into you,' he'd said in the deep voice that had always melted her heart. Still did.

Damn him. It would be so easy—too easy—to tell him how she felt and not let the past get in the way.

But every time she'd thought they might be able to do just that, her chest would tighten with fear. What if she gave in and it all backfired? She should never have got so close to him. All her fault.

'You hanging around here all night?' Nicolas asked from the doorway.

'Not likely,' she muttered. 'Adding some notes about my last patient, is all.'

'See you tomorrow then.' Nicolas didn't move away, stood watching her with something like hope in those blue eyes she had recalled every night when she lay in bed with the light off and sleep taking its time to envelop her.

'I'll be here. Are you working every day this week?'

'Yes. It means others can spend time with their families.' And he didn't have one. Even so, that was kind.

Not that she was surprised. 'I'm baking brownies tonight to bring in tomorrow.' It was her birthday, but no one needed to know. She'd pretend it was for those who had to work between the two holiday weekends.

He licked his lips. Lips she could all too easily recall on her skin as they made out. 'Then there's nothing that'll keep me away.'

Watching him smile was undoing her resolve, making her flush with need.

Please go, Nicolas. I don't need you here, reminding me so clearly of what I'm missing out on.

Turning back to the screen, she finished with her last patient's notes and closed the computer down. She couldn't sit here staring at the blank screen for ever, though. Standing up, she reached for her keys and turned around.

Nicolas had gone.

Relief vied with disappointment. They'd not talked about anything except work, but she'd enjoyed every moment. Face it. Just sharing the same air as him turned her on, and made her feel she might be making a huge mistake trying to keep him at arm's length. Seeing his eyes lighten, his long fingers when he rubbed his wrist, the vee at the front of his scrubs, dragging her gaze downward to what she knew was behind his clothes—all added up to the love she wasn't ready to acknowledge openly. She needed more time to think about what she was prepared to take a chance on. Her emotions were taking a roller coaster ride—a ride with no end in sight.

Nicolas drove home with his head full of Claire.

Claire concentrating on helping the elderly lady who'd broken three fingers when she'd closed her car door with one hand still holding the framework.

Claire smiling tiredly as she stood up from her desk and rubbed her lower back before going to get her next patient.

Claire giving him a surprised smile when he placed a mug of coffee on her desk because she'd been too busy to get her own. Her surprise had stung, but then she wasn't used to people looking out for her. She'd once said it was one of the best things to come out of her move north so far. Everyone was friendly and caring. Her life in Dunedin must've been bleak. The little she'd mentioned about her mother suggested there hadn't been a lot of love going around.

Except for Mia. Claire loved that little girl so much. It was beautiful to witness. Could she love someone else half as much? Him? Because he loved her so much he ached twenty-four-seven.

The four-wheel drive slowed. His foot had slipped off the accelerator. He wanted Claire to love him. Of course he did. That was half the problem. He wanted her to share his life, and that meant she had to love him. She'd become remote at work, talking to him only when needed, smiling softly but not as whole-heartedly as she used to. He missed her so much it was as though his world had fallen apart.

The back wheels spun as he accelerated away, trying to outrun his thoughts. He did want Claire at his side. Long-term. Absolutely. For ever? That was the rub. How did anyone know the answer to that? He'd loved Valerie, believing it was for ever, and that had turned into a train wreck. Whatever he had going with Claire, they needed to talk. Not about patients but about themselves.

The entrance to his property appeared and he turned sharply. Hadn't seen it coming, been too deep in thought about Claire. Parking by the shed, he went to check the water metre and make sure the vines had had enough water during the particularly hot day.

A cold beer while he cooked a steak for dinner was next on his list. It had to be at least twenty-five degrees out here still. A hot night lay ahead. Not caused by Claire's gorgeous body lying entangled with his either.

Make that two cold beers. Something had to cool him down. If at all possible.

It was after midnight when he eventually managed to grab a few hours' sleep, and he was already hot under the collar within minutes of arriving at the emergency clinic next morning. Even hotter below the waistband of his uniform when he saw Claire talking to Ryan.

Claire. Filling out her version of the uniform with curves in all the right places. Wearing her hair loose for a change, curls tucked behind her ears. A tight smile appeared as she placed the container of brownies on the bench in the tearoom. Tiredness evident in her eyes.

Only Claire could make him feel this hot and flustered and wanting to scoop her into his arms and hug away her obvious exhaustion. Exhaustion similar to that dragging at his shoulders.

'Morning.' He nodded at the brownies. 'That looks delicious even this early in the day.'

'Do we have to wait until tea break?' Ryan took the lid off the container and inhaled the chocolate aroma. 'This beats what I had for breakfast.'

'Help yourself,' Claire replied with a small

chuckle. 'But do leave some for everyone else.'
As she made mugs of tea, she said, 'I hope
we're not too busy today.'

He hoped they were flat-out and then the
time would speed past.

'Here.' She handed him a mug and picked up
one for herself before heading out of the room.

Nicolas watched her go, her back straight,
and no doubt a forced smile on the face he
couldn't see. She was trying too hard to fit in
today. What had happened? A bad night trying to sleep? Or had Mia kept her awake? Or
was she feeling confused and frustrated about
him and them? Like he was? He followed her
into the consultation room.

'You okay?'

'Why wouldn't I be?'

He should walk out of here, go back to the
tearoom and drink his tea. Instead he continued. 'You seem tired and look like you don't
want to be here.'

Her eyes widened. 'Great. Guess I went a
little light on the make-up this morning.'

'Cut it out, Claire. I'm concerned that you're
all right. That's all.' That wasn't the half of it
but he wasn't saying any more here.

She dropped onto the chair in front of the
computer, tea splashing onto her hand. 'Sorry.

I could do with a little more sleep, but it's not happening so I'd better get on with my day.'

'Where's Mia today?'

'Jess and Joachim offered to look after her. She gets on well with one of their daughters so they figure having Mia there gives them some free time.'

Didn't sound as though there were any problems with Mia then.

'It's good how she's making new friends so easily. But then she is a right little charmer.'

Finally a real smile appeared. 'She's always been like that. It does make life easier when it comes to taking up offers of staying with other people when I'm working.'

This from the woman who'd mentioned setting up her own general practice. There'd be even less free time to spend with her daughter. Not that he was mentioning that at the moment either. That smile was worth keeping in place.

'She's a lot like Michelle, very easy to get on with and happy to join in all the fun.'

'I won't mind if Mia is as good as Michelle when she's a teenager.'

'Think I said once before, don't even start worrying about those years. Make the most of this phase while you've got it.'

'Good idea.' Unfortunately Claire's smile dipped.

His suggestion not so easy to stick to? The sound of the front door being unlocked and people entering reached him. Saved him from further turmoil.

'Here we go.' He headed for the triage office, noting only three adults queuing at Reception. A quiet start to the day. Damn.

Twelve hours stretched ahead. Right now he'd prefer to be inundated with patients than sitting around, fully aware of Claire every second of those hours. His hand tightened, loosened. They had to talk, to get this out in the open and deal with their differences. Had to. Not at work though. There were other staff members who'd overhear them, and patients would still come through the door to interrupt when they least needed to be. Besides, the last thing Claire looked as if she might want to do was have a deep and meaningful conversation with him any time soon.

'I'm just calling into the medical centre to get my phone, Mia.' She'd left it behind last night and by the time she'd realised she was at home and couldn't be bothered going back to get it.

'Is Nicolas there? I want to see him.' Mia had got over her upsetting moment with him in a short time, as she had when Santa hadn't promised a hug. He hadn't turned into an ogre after all.

If only I could move on as easily.

'Yes, he is.' The car park was full. What was going on? It was New Year's Eve and the staff on duty hadn't expected to be busy. 'We'll have to walk a little way, Mia.'

They were barely in the front door when Ryan saw her and said, 'Claire, am I glad you're here.'

'What's going on?' The waiting room was over-full and a quick look to the room with beds and monitors showed the same.

'ED can't take any more patients. There was a multi car accident at the intersection of Jackson's and Rapaura Roads, with multiple patients in serious conditions. We're taking the backlog, and minutes ago a family was brought in needing urgent attention.'

'I'm available.' How could she walk out of here while everyone needed all the help they could get?

'I'll look after Mia,' Diane, the receptionist, called. 'Come on, Mia. You can help me in here.'

'Okay. Can I type on your computer?'

Claire laughed. 'Good luck, Diane. You've got your hands full.'

'So have you.'

'Where do you want me, Ryan?'

'In with the family that's just been brought in. Nicolas is already there. He'll fill you in. I've got a child with possible appendicitis in my room.'

'Claire, good to see you.' Nicolas stepped up the moment she entered the room, strain evident in his eyes. 'First, John Cooper.' He indicated the man writhing on a bed as a nurse tried to attach monitors to his bare chest. 'This family were out in their alloy dinghy when a rogue wave hit, tossing them all out. John took a hit on the shoulder and back, but managed to get to Troy.' Another nod at a small boy on another bed being cuddled by a woman, presumably his mother. 'Troy took in a lot of water and stopped breathing. Fortunately bystanders rushed to take over, forcing Troy to cough the water out and then got him breathing. This is Pip Cooper, and this little girl is Gina. She was very lucky and only got wet. And a big fright.'

Claire shook her head, trying to absorb everything while moving towards John. The woman looked shocked but in control, though she did wince when Troy moved. 'Where are you at with everyone?' she asked Nicolas.

'I'm checking Troy out. We've wrapped him in blankets to raise his temperature. He has mild hypothermia. Can you examine John?

He's got an injury to his lower leg where he thinks the propeller might've hit.'

She shuddered at what might've happened. 'Why isn't there another doctor in here?'

'Ryan was, but then he got called to a more urgent case.'

More urgent? Then they were really up for an intense time. Claire snapped gloves on, and put a hand on John's chest. He was shivering from top to toe. 'You need blankets too. John, I'm Claire, a doctor.' She looked to Karen, the nurse. 'Need a hand?' They needed those monitors doing their job.

'Yep.'

'Leave me. Look after Troy. He needs you first. I'll be all right,' John growled. 'He's only little, he needs you.'

'Nicolas is doing everything I would do. We need to make you warm again, and to check you over for injuries.' Blood had soaked the bed from John's lower leg. 'And stop the bleeding and see what other damage has been done.'

'I don't care. See to Troy.'

'He's being looked after.'

'What about Gina? Is she all right?'

'She's fine,' Nicolas called.

Pip appeared beside Claire, her arms empty of her son. 'John, please calm down, darling. Troy is in good hands. Nicolas knows what he's doing, and Troy is alert now. You saved him. Now lie back and get patched up yourself.'

John locked his gaze on his wife, and slowly the tension left him. 'If you say so.'

Between them, Claire and Karen got the last of the wet clothes off John. While Karen dried him with a towel, Claire examined his leg. 'This needs a lot of sutures, but I think you've escaped serious damage.' She could see the bones and neither had been chipped. 'We'll get an X-ray to make sure there isn't a fracture but I think there'd be other damage if there was.' A spinning propeller wouldn't make a clean fracture.

The door kept opening and closing behind her as Karen came and went with blankets and other equipment.

Nicolas joined her. 'Karen will watch over Troy. I'll help you.'

'I need to look at his back where you mentioned he was struck by the boat.'

'You hear that, John?' Nicolas wasn't wasting any time. 'Claire and I are going to roll you onto your side. Don't try and help, or resist us. It will cause more pain.'

His tight nod obviously caused him pain as a groan escaped him. 'You sure Troy's all right?'

'Yes. He's going to need pampering for a day or two, and then he'll be charging around like nothing happened.' Nicolas's hands were firm on John's hip and leg while Claire held his shoulder. 'One, two, three.'

They had him where they wanted.

A massive bruise covered most of his back and neck. 'Why didn't someone put a neck brace on?'

'The family was brought in by those same bystanders who saved Troy. They went to ED but the orderly sent them across to us. By then John had been moving around a lot. I did suggest it but Ryan didn't think it necessary.'

'He's probably right.' Though she'd have erred on the side of caution. Then she did that all the time about most things. A quick glance at Nicolas. Including him. Mostly him. Then, inexplicably, she relaxed some.

Nicolas had things under control. He was applying the monitors that John had refused. He wasn't fazed by the trauma.

'Have any painkillers been administered?' she asked.

'A dose of Tramadol about two minutes before you arrived.'

'John, what's your pain level on a scale of one to ten?'

'Four.'

'I'll get something stronger,' she said, having seen the sharp spears of pain that hit John every time he moved. 'You're in more pain than you're letting on.'

'I'll get it. What do you want?' Nicolas asked.

Claire told him, and continued checking John for further injuries. Bruises and swelling were appearing all over his upper torso. 'Did the boat hit you more than once?'

'I can't answer that. I felt an almighty whack and don't remember much afterwards other than the need to get to Troy. I could see Pip had Gina.'

'Is John going to be all right?' Pip asked, watching every touch Claire made, her face strained.

'He needs a scan and X-rays. His head has taken a hard knock, leaving the bone soft in one spot. His shoulder isn't moving in its socket. Whether it was dislocated then became wedged awkwardly in the socket will come to light in the X-ray.' She continued outlining the injuries and what would happen next.

Make that whenever Theatre and surgeons, plus Radiology were available. The people from the car crash were already in the queue. Blenheim Hospital was showing how small it really was.

Time dragged on. Claire and Nicolas treated John as much as possible. She stitched his calf muscle back together while Nicolas swabbed the site regularly and passed across whatever she needed. A team. Whatever happened between them, they had this. Which could mean a lot for the future if she toughened up and made a go for him.

Troy was moved to the paediatric ward. Pip went along to see him settled, then returned to her husband's side. 'Where's Gina?'

Claire took her arm gently. 'Come with me.' She led Pip to Reception. 'Look at her.'

'She's having fun,' Pip gasped, then swatted her face with the back of her hand.

Mia and Gina were on the floor, backs against the wall, playing a game on a tablet, giggling as they took turns tapping the screen to make something happen.

'Who's the other girl?'

'Mia. My daughter.' Her pride and joy was helping Gina get through a harrowing experience.

'She's lovely.' Tears were streaming down Pip's face. The events of the day were finally catching up. 'Gina is John's daughter. I had Troy before I met him. But no one would know that. He treats him as his son, and today was no exception. He saved our boy. He put him first.'

Claire couldn't help herself. She wrapped her arms around Pip and hugged her. This woman had what she hoped for, love for herself and her children.

'He's one of a kind,' Pip sniffed as she stepped back.

No, there was another man like John. He just needed to accept she loved him enough for both of them. Of course she had to tell him first.

She took Pip's arm again. 'Right, everyone else is being taken care of, so now it's your turn to be examined.'

'You noticed?'

Hard not to. 'Your upper left arm. You can't lift it. You grimaced with pain every time you moved Troy. I suspect a fracture.'

'Two fractures within an inch of each other,' Nicolas read from the screen an hour later. 'I'll sort the cast when you've talked to her.' He stood up. 'Then you'd better take Mia and get out of here while you can.'

'As long as I'm not needed, I will.' Mia had been a champ but almost three hours was a long time. 'I think she deserves fried chicken and chips.'

'Don't we all?'

Which gave her an idea. 'Come on, Mia. You and I have something to do.' How many pieces of chicken would she need to order to feed all the staff?

* * *

'Thank goodness that's over.' Claire tossed her keys on the bench and opened all the windows to let the stifling air out. Working with Nicolas had been good for the first time since Christmas. Calming really. Rejuvenating. The last days she'd worked had been draining as she continuously fought the urge to wrap her arms around him and tell him he was special. Trying hard not to admit she was struggling with not sharing time together outside of the clinic had sucked what little energy she had out of her. Today had been different. Today they'd been connected, each knowing what was required for the patient without saying a word. Each knowing the other would give everything possible to help their patients.

How was she going to cope next year? A new year was beginning in less than eight hours. Fifty-two weeks to spend a lot of days working alongside Nicolas.

'Mummy, Nicolas is here.'

'What? Where?'

'His car's in the drive.'

How had she missed that?

'Hello, Nicolas. Have you come to see Mummy?' Mia had run to open the door.

'Yes, I have. And you too.' He was standing tall, tension in his shoulders and his face.

'I'm going to play with my kitchen. I'll make you some tea.'

Claire smiled. 'Come in, Nicolas,' she said.

A bottle hung from his hand. 'Would you like some wine?'

'I'd prefer to talk.'

Some of the tension relaxed. 'Yes, we need to, but a glass of wine with that won't hurt.'

Spinning around, Claire went into the kitchen and, for something to do with her suddenly tense hands, opened a cupboard for some glasses. She filled the glasses too much. Didn't care. They were going to talk. She sipped the wine, needing something to make her feel good.

Give over. Nicolas makes you feel good.

Even though she didn't know where they stood, he made her feel she wasn't so alone any more. He set her heart racing and her blood warming. He made her realise she could put her heart out there and take a chance on him. She had to, or regret it for ever.

She passed him a glass. 'How's our family?' Work was not what she'd been about to mention. Nothing like it. Her self-protection mode was firmly in place.

'John's doing fine, but they're keeping him in overnight for monitoring. Troy's been shifted to the same room so he doesn't wake up frightened after what happened.'

'They're all very close.' *Go on. Ask him. Drop the façade, Claire. Be the woman you so want to be.* 'You understood John's relationship to Troy right from the get-go, didn't you?' This was going the long way round but something said it was the right way.

Those intense blue eyes locked on her. 'Yes.'

'You'd do the same for Mia.'

'Yes.'

Her head tipped back and she stared at the ceiling, willing the sudden rare tears not to drip down her face. Nicolas would've risked his life to save her daughter. He was the all or nothing kind of man, and she'd go for all with him.

Swiping at her face with her hand, she placed her glass on the counter and looked at him. 'Absolutely. I know that. It's one reason I can't live without you, Nicolas. The other is I love you. As in love everything about you. Enough to want a future together. More children with you.' When she finally let go, there was no stopping her. Because if she didn't get it all out there now she might never manage it.

The silence was deafening. He looked stunned.

Had she really got this so wrong? It was

always going to be a risk, remember? She'd fronted up, and if she'd made a mistake then she'd live with it. She loved Nicolas. If he didn't love her, then so be it.

'Claire—'

'Nicolas—'

They stopped and locked eyes with each other.

He nodded. 'You were going to say?'

Again her lips trembled as she tried to smile. 'I...' Her breasts rose on a sharp intake of air and dropped slowly as she exhaled. 'I think I said it all. I love you.'

Claire loves me.

Nicolas stared at the glass in her shaking hand. She'd said she loved him. Showed she had a lot more guts than he did when there was a lot more for her to lose. But he wasn't surprised. Had known it all along. One of the reasons he loved her.

Moving beside her, he took the glass from her cold hands and wound his fingers around them. 'I've missed you these past days, even when we've been in the same building, working together on the same patient. Today not so much because we were as one.'

She didn't move, not a blink.

'You've come to mean so much to me it's

been hard to focus on anything but what we've been missing out on.'

Teeth dug into her bottom lip.

Get on with it, man.

'But—'

Claire jerked backwards. Her hands slipped out of his.

Reaching for her, he said, 'Sorry. I'll start again.' This shouldn't be so hard. But it wasn't something he was used to saying, though the words were waiting, ready to spill from his lips and put his heart out there for whatever Claire wanted to do with it. 'I've told you I've been married and that it fell apart against my wishes. I have moved on, but there's been a certain amount of fear I might be hurt if I fell in love again. That has kept me wary, as I imagine your past has you.'

She blinked, nodded once.

'The thing is, Claire, from the moment I met you, no, make that from when I first laid eyes on you at the kids' Santa party, I've been fighting to hold onto the caution. I've wanted to let it go and fly high with you. I'd get in the car to come see you and then I'd remember what being dumped felt like and I'd go back home.'

'So why are you here now?' The hope was returning to her eyes.

'Simple. I've fallen in love with you, and I want to spend the rest of my life with you. Of course, Mia's a part of that picture. If you'll have me.'

She stared at him for so long he thought his heart was going to break into a million pieces.

Finally, 'How do you know it will be for ever?'

'I don't. Nor do you. But if we don't try, then we've definitely lost out. I'd prefer to get on with living and loving you, and do everything within my power to make it work right on into old age.' Had he made her see he did love her? That she was the most important person to him? 'Claire, I—'

Her finger pressed into his lips. 'My turn.' A smile lit up her face, and made him relax a teeny bit. 'I understand. I've struggled to accept a man will love me enough to be there for ever. Because of that, I probably hold back on my feelings too much. But when you came along there was no stopping me wanting to know more and more about you, to be with you. I have fallen in love with you. Nicolas, I love you so much I can't put it into words. I can't imagine the pain of not sharing my life with you.'

'Then you can stop worrying because I'm here for you, with you, for ever.' Only then did he do what he'd wanted to do for days. Taking her in his arms, he kissed her. And then some more.

When they finally came up for air, Claire laughed. 'I'd better check up on Mia.'

Taking her hand, he walked inside and stopped to grin at the sight of Mia busy making pretend tea. 'That's love. That's what we've got.'

'Only better.'

'Will you two move in with me?' he asked, surprising himself, since he hadn't thought this far ahead, fully expecting to have been walking down the path to his vehicle alone by now.

'I'd like that.' Claire grinned. 'Here's to the new year and new beginnings. Just what I'd wished for.'

It felt right. But not perfect. Turning to face her full-on, Nicolas reached for Claire's hands. 'Claire McAlpine, will you marry me? Have more children with me?'

A smile to remember for always took over her mouth, her face, her eyes. 'Yes to both, Nicolas Reid. Yes.' She leaned in to kiss him. 'Yes,' she whispered against his mouth. 'Yes.'

'Mummy, why are you kissing Nicolas?'

They leaned back in each other's arms and

looked at Mia, her eyes wide as she stared at them.

'Because I love him, Mia.'

'Do you love Mummy, Nicolas?'

'Yes, little one, I do. So much that we're going to get married.'

Mia charged them, arms outstretched. 'Can I come too?'

'We wouldn't go without you,' he managed around the sudden lump in his throat.

'Can I have a cuddle, Nicolas?'

Tears spilled down his face. 'Oh, sweetheart. I've got so many hugs waiting for you, you won't believe it.' He swept Mia up into his arms. Then pulled Claire in to join them. 'I love you both.'

Claire whispered, 'Do you know what this means, Mia? We're going to live with Nicolas, and we're going to be a family.'

'Is he going to be my dad?' Serious eyes looked from Claire and fixed on him.

Nicolas felt his heart squeeze painfully. 'Yes, I am. Is that okay?'

'Give me another cuddle and I'll say yes.'

Tears slipped down his cheeks as he obliged this lovely little girl who'd once asked for something he hadn't thought he could deliver, and now found he could—easily.

'Cuddle number two.'
Claire hugged them both. 'Happy New Year.'
Yeah. Bring it on. Happy New Year.

* * * * *

If you enjoyed this story, check out
these other great reads from
Sue MacKay

Stranded with the Paramedic
Fling with Her Long-Lost Surgeon
Their Second Chance in ER
From Best Friends to I Do?

All available now!